ECHOES THROUGH TIME

HINDSIGHT

MARY TURNER THOMSON

Published by

The Book Whisperers
community . interest . company

ISBN (Paperback) - 978-1-909797-90-1
ISBN (Hardback) -   978-1-909797-91-8

www.thebookwhisperers.com

To Jon,
Who first took me to Tynemouth Priory
And who left this life too soon.

Jonathon Neal - 1964-2018

Prologue:
"I love you"

Catherine choked on the laughter that had moments before been exploding out of her. She couldn't help but wonder: had he really said those three little words? She froze – her smile fading. He had blurted it out so casually. And so publicly! Surely, he meant to say he loved her sense of humour, or that he enjoyed the sarky comment she just made? No doubt he was already regretting the words and having made them sound so intimate.

A whispering voice inside her head cast a shadow of doubt, suggesting that this all seemed too perfect, too beyond her usual experience. This inner voice stirred a subtle unease, and a persistent inkling of scepticism nagged at the edges of her consciousness.

She gave herself a shake. Of course he didn't love her – it was not possible. She was, quite simply, unlovable. One day he would see that and want nothing more to do with her. She brushed the thoughts aside, deciding to pretend she hadn't heard his confession. Easier to dodge the moment than confront whatever that lingering unease was.

By the time she dared to look up, John was pointing at the underground map overhead working out the number of stops until they arrived at Tynemouth. The metro train jostled them both, and John put his other arm around her waist to support her.

Catherine took in his rugged face and strong rugby player physique that could rival a Hollywood star - she knew that he was out of her league. She also knew she liked him from the way her pulse sped up every time he was near. She even had a strong, and rather irrational, desire to crawl inside his skin. So what was stopping her from saying those three little words back?

"This is our stop," John said, "I'm so excited to show you Tynemouth Priory, you're going to love it."

Love. That word again. Its repetition startled Catherine, like an accusation. He couldn't mean it, not when it came to her. She was fooling herself to think otherwise.

Catherine turned her attention to Tynemouth Priory instead. She was curious what he found so attractive about a ruin by the sea. For some reason, John had thought it would make a good day out and so she had gone along with the idea, and now she let him lead her off the metro and up the stairs to the streets above.

They stepped out of the metro station and walked hand in hand around a slow bend in the road.

With each step Catherine felt more and more strange.

She couldn't put her finger on it but alarm bells were ringing in her head. The odd sensation intensified, and Catherine looked up and around at her unfamiliar surroundings in confusion. Then, as they reached the main street in Tynemouth, Catherine stopped abruptly, sucking in a sharp breath.

She stared open mouthed at the red and white brick buildings on either side of the wide road. Each house rose to a different height and size, with pillared doorways and bay windows giving off the relaxed air of a seaside town.

Catherine's heartbeat quickened as half-forgotten memories clicked into place. She knew this place. She had been here before. "What the ...?" Her mind rebelled, even as her heart flooded with recognition.

"What's up Cat?"

Catherine glanced around. For a fraction of a second she had entirely forgotten that John was there. She seemed totally disconnected from him, from everything, even though her hand was still in his. The sensation disconcerted her.

"I know this place. I've been here before..." She struggled to articulate the impossibility.

"It's déjà vu," John shrugged as he let go of her hand and took a sausage roll out of his backpack, taking a bite. "Lots of people get it."

"What?" Catherine felt rather irritated not only to be dismissed but also because he was speaking with his mouth full.

"You know - the feeling you've been somewhere before?"

"I know what it is!" She tried to keep the sharp edge out of her voice – it reminded her too much of her grandmother's scolding tone, "No, it's not that." Then more softly she added, "I feel the place is familiar, I remember being here ... remember what I did, where I went, and what I saw. It isn't a flash, it's ... a whole experience." Catherine looked back at the street ahead of them – she could hear the echoes of laughter.

The memories flooded in at the first sight of the town centre. Impossible though it was, she recognised the street in front of her. Remembered walking down the pavements on a day there many years before. It played in her mind like an old movie – flashing snapshots of smiling people, her laughing, intense happiness and a connection she didn't recognise in herself. The streets were quite unremarkable and yet they made an unmistakable pattern in her mind.

John's brow furrowed, but he didn't dismiss her outburst. "But you said that you hadn't been to Tynemouth before."

3

Still gazing down the street taking in every familiar detail, Catherine replied, "I haven't. I'd never been out of Scotland before coming to uni. I wasn't allowed to go anywhere." She shrugged, and put a smile on her face before adding, "It is what made coming to Newcastle Uni such an incredible adventure."

"You'd never even been on holiday?" John seemed surprised.

"My grandmother thought them an extravagance that we couldn't afford. I never even went for a sleepover," then added under her breath, "not that anyone ever asked me."

"Really?" John looked surprised. "That seems a bit sad."

Catherine shrugged and looked up at him, "My grandmother was pretty strict that way. It was all *study hard* and *good manners*, and life would start after I left school, kind of stuff. She wasn't so bad, always had my best interests at heart – just wasn't the sociable type." Catherine looked back at Tynemouth again, struggling to connect the streets she now remembered with the ones in front of her. "This is all crazy. I can't have been here. I simply can't. I didn't go on any school trips. I was never allowed. It's not even like it's that long ago – I am only 19 now so it can only have been 5 or 6 years ago. If I'd travelled here, it would have been a huge deal and I would have remembered the name when you mentioned it."

"Well, it has to be déjà vu then," John said as he offered her some the sausage roll.

Catherine shook her head, so he shoved the last of it into his mouth and took her hand again as they started to walk down the street.

Catherine wondered whether he thought her mad. Had he taken her hand because he thought her unstable? She needed to prove to him that her new-found memories were real. She remembered it all so well, although she was certain that she'd never been there before. What's more, it meant a huge deal to

4

her. This was a place that she cherished; it had a special place already firmly rooted in her heart.

"Ok, so tell me what you remember?" John gestured to the whole length of Tynemouth's High Street. The road was wide enough to have two rows of cars parked in the centre, bumper-to-bumper, leaving the moving traffic to go one way on either side.

"I remember this street – but last time I saw a funfair here. There were no cars parked in the middle of the road then, just fairground rides, a roundabout, candyfloss stores and stuff."

"I've never seen a fair in the High Street before, but then I've only been coming here a few years," said John.

"Well, it was here in my memory. That can't be déjà vu then, can it?"

"I don't think so." John frowned.

More and more details came flooding in as Catherine's memory of the place came to the surface.

They walked down the high street, towards the sea. Catherine straining her neck right and left as she spotted places she recognised and patterns that clicked in her mind.

"We watched the horses in the merry-go-round – just here. There were stalls selling crafts all along the street, and there were even people doing puppet shows. We weren't there to see the fair, I knew that, but I wanted to stay and see it anyway. Then I was asked to come away and followed the group as they walked down to the Priory."

"The group? What about details, do you remember what you were wearing for instance, or who you were with?"

Catherine pictured herself, she could see the blue jeans and a plain white t-shirt that she wore. She was quite young - an early teenager maybe. She had a page-boy haircut which she had hated but it was the only cut her grandmother, Eve, knew how to do - hairdressers being another *frivolous* expense. It was the style she sported until she got old enough to let it grow out. She did not consider it a good look, and Catherine thought it best not to mention it.

"I was with a bunch of people, I can picture them, but I don't recognise any of them ... I can roughly see what they look like, but I don't know who they are." She remembered feeling oddly comfortable in their company and strangely confident in her place amongst them. She'd been happy there, whereas, in reality, she had always felt like the outsider, the studious loner that everyone pretty much ignored. "After wandering through the fair and down the High Street, we arrived here."

They stopped at the end of the road directly across from the main gates of Tynemouth Priory. A deep dry moat-like incline surrounded the fortified outcrop, so the road had to snake around to circumvent it. It came to a stop directly in front of the imposing towers on either side of the medieval gates.

John started to turn to the left, but Catherine caught his arm. "We went down to the beach on the south side of the rock first." She pointed down the road. "We found a small beach in a bay and ran around on the sand, messing about. I took my jeans off to paddle but my t-shirt got wet through from splashing in the waves. It was a warm day but staying wet was getting very cold. So, we went up to the Priory, and the man who took the entrance fees very kindly gave me a t-shirt from the shop to wear. He didn't even charge us for it."

Catherine led John down the road as it curved around the south side of the cliff, and the small bay came into view – just as Catherine had described it. She stood looking at the scene and Catherine again sensed the strange dual feeling of both remembering a place and seeing it for the first time. Like her heart and her head were arguing with each other. They stood for a moment looking at the waves caressing the sandy shore and Catherine could hear the laughter echoing in her ears as she vividly pictured the group of long-gone teenagers chasing each other around.

"Then we went into the Priory," Catherine turned to look up the incline and noticed a shiver rush over her. The ruined Priory stood on top of imposing 150ft cliffs on three sides. The only access was via the road and dry moat at the end of the main street. Something about approaching the gate made her heart quicken and it became harder to breathe. She shook it off and walked back up the road to the main gates with determination.

"Hold on!" John said as he scrambled to keep up with her.

Once inside the Priory, the memories were even more vivid. At each step, she described what was around the next corner before it came into view – and on each occasion she was correct.

She remembered the staircase that led nowhere just inside the gatehouse; the ruined abbey walls which overshadowed the impossibly small stone coffins. She even remembered and described various gravestones which had intricate pagan symbols, some of which were being eaten away by the salty sea winds.

John became more and more intrigued, asking questions and looking carefully at everything that Catherine showed him.

As they sat cross legged on the grass near the edge of the cliff looking out at the view of the North Sea, Catherine looked at her boyfriend a little more closely. She was so grateful that he hadn't dismissed her memories as fantasy or delusion. Another person might have thought her mad. He was definitely too good a person for her and she was glad they had moved past the awkwardness of his declaration in the Metro. When John looked up and caught her eye, she continued to tell him what she could remember.

"It was a gorgeous day, with no clouds in the sky. We laid blankets out on the ground and had quartered white bread sandwiches with cucumber and white cheese on them – over there," she pointed to a grassy area beyond the broken-down walls. "After the picnic, I went exploring the ruins with an older girl. She had long hair which fell loosely around her shoulders, and for some reason I felt very close to her. I even remember playing with her hair."

Nothing of real consequence happened – it was just a day out - but she didn't remember anything about how she travelled there or how they left. She didn't even remember any of the people and could only describe the one girl with whom she had been exploring the grounds.

The memories were so clear, so vivid in their detail and complexity that it baffled Catherine. As she led John around the ruins, he seemed to become more convinced and intrigued with each revelation - though Catherine did wonder if he was placating her. On only one occasion her predicted layout was incorrect and it was one that was the most vivid to Catherine. She remembered a cave entrance that she had explored. However, the cave that she had investigated was not there at all - only an ordinary ruined medieval wall where the cavern entrance had been. The fact that it was not there seemed alien to Catherine, like part of a photograph had been scratched out.

Catherine was still distracted by the memories that evening when John cooked her dinner - she found the sensations hard to shake. There had to be a rational reason for the random recollections she had uncovered. She'd never been out of Edinburgh until she finally finished school, packed up all her belongings and moved down to Newcastle - getting a job in a bar before uni had started. She'd waited long enough for her life to start and was impatient to get on with it. The freedom was delicious, and she didn't miss her family home at all. Her grandmother, Eve, had made it clear that her job of raising Catherine was now finished, and the rest of the young woman's life was up to her. Lost in thought she pushed the food around her plate with her fork.

"Cat, did you hear me?"

"Huh?" Catherine looked up into John's intense eyes as he reached out and took both her hands between the dirty plates of pasta. It pulled her out of her reverie.

"I said, I love you, Cat."

Catherine paused and then leaned over to kiss him. There was no avoiding it this time. She had never been told those words before today and was left with a profound sense of his delusion. It was only a matter of time before he realised his mistake – and when he did, he would likely want nothing more to do with her. She smiled as sweetly as she was able and kissed him again, then she repeated the words back - like she had seen people do in films. He seemed to be happy with that and Catherine knew that she had done well – even if she was rather bemused by the whole situation.

She poured herself a large glass of wine and drank it, fast. She needed to numb the rising feelings that threatened to overwhelm her. The day had been a kaleidoscope of memory and emotion which seemed to be opening a door in her mind – one which she was determined should stay stoically shut. Another couple of glasses and she was numbed enough to feel normal again, albeit a bit drunk. Having never had a drink before arriving in Newcastle nine months before, she had little tolerance for it. However, with the memories and the feelings now suppressed she was able to go to bed with John and relax into his arms. After, she lay with her back to his belly as he wrapped himself around her and fell asleep.

She stood on the edge, with her back to the cliff. The dawn had broken and the rosy light illuminated the scene around her.

She shivered with fear but then a stronger emotion tugged at her as well. She pulled herself up to her full hight, tilting her face up to the sky – powerful and serene – something unfamiliar. She closed her eyes and smiled. Then she stepped backwards off the cliff.

Having launched herself into the space beyond she plummeted downwards. Feeling weightless and breathless. Her clothes billowed and flapped in the drumming wind. Her heart beat wildly as she witnessed the world she knew blur into the distance. She didn't scream. She experienced no fear, just a profound sense of acceptance. Then she smashed heavily on the rocks.

Pain exploded through her body - but it faded quickly.

The smell of raw sharp seaweed washed over her and its tendrils caressed her skin. The gulls were calling out for her. And then the ocean pulled her broken body under the waves and into the waiting arms of death.

Catherine gasped for air as she sat up in bed and clamped her hand over her mouth. She needed to control her breathing – slow it down. She froze in place, pressing her hand over her lips as she cautiously breathed out through her nose. At the same time, she took a furtive glance to check that John was still asleep beside her. She watched his chest rise and fall a couple of times before she was sure he was still oblivious - and only then did she release her hand and start to breath normally again.

The dream was no stranger, but this was the first time she'd experienced it with someone in the bed beside her. She didn't want to have to explain what it all meant. Suicidally throwing herself off a clifftop would sound morbid - particularly after the romantic evening that John had gone to so much effort to provide.

The dream wasn't ominous to her at all – it never was. Sometimes she took flight and became a bird, flying free over the wide ocean. She would feel the feathers sprout down her neck and along her arms as she took wing. The wind holding her up was a joy that defied explanation. Most times though, she fell. And would spend her last moments paralysed on the rocks as the waves washed over her. Yet always she was left with a feeling of gratitude for her life, something that was not so familiar in her waking existence.

The dream was intense and personal, and way too intimate to share. John would think it a nightmare, but he would be wrong.

She lay down again, taking care not to wake John, and closed her eyes - certain that she could still hear the sound of the gulls as she drifted back to sleep.

~ 1 ~

Falling

"This may well have been a very bad idea," Catherine said to herself as the flat door opened and the sound of raucous laughter echoed down the tenement stairs. The work colleagues who had persuaded her to come along to the party vanished inside the moment the door opened, leaving Catherine standing on the doorstep wondering whether she could make a break for it. She imagined herself leaping down the stairs three at a time - and no-one would be the wiser.

However, the host had other ideas. "Come on in! The more the merrier!" he said as he directed her to the kitchen where the bar was.

Catherine had to admit that the flat was gorgeous; a Georgian central Edinburgh apartment flaunting its high ceilings and huge rooms. It was crowded with people in their mid-to-late twenties – Catherine's peers, although she never felt one of them. She hadn't loved parties like this at uni and was no keener now that she was supposedly a grown-up young professional.

On her way to the kitchen she could hear loud music coming from a large bay-windowed living room. She took a peek in passing and noticed a DJ and people were dancing in the middle of the room. In the kitchen was a bar and a buffet.

Groups of people talked and laughed everywhere that she looked.

What on earth was she doing there? Watching people who were drunk and wasting a lot of time and energy talking about nothing? She'd decided to stay for a little while, for appearance's sake, so that her work colleagues didn't think she was anti-social. After all you can't get ahead if people don't like you. So, she smiled and was polite, pretended to be having a good time whilst she watched the clock to see when she might be able to escape back home to a good book and a whiskey or two. She poured herself a large glass of white wine to dull the pain of the social event, whilst she looked around the room.

At least there was some decent eye candy there. It had been four years since university had ended, and her last serious relationship, with John, had ground to a halt. Maybe it was time to think about doing more than just dating again. One chap over by the fireplace was very attractive. Tall, handsome with a cheeky twinkle in his eye which only added to his charm. Like something out of a story book – too good to be true. He had something magnetic about him, as if he was the very centre of the room.

The man glanced in her direction and caught her looking. Catherine jerked nervously – she only just managed to stop her drink from spilling and looked away.

"Damn!" she muttered.

She pulled herself together and could hear her grandmother's sharp tongue in her head. *'What on earth is wrong with you, he's only a man, and now he's seen you he will be laughing at your obvious lust.'*

She decided to focus on who else was in the room. There were the guys from work, all drinking far too much ... there were lots of people she didn't know ... and she found she was looking in his direction again. Thankfully, he was now looking the other way.

What was it about the way he was standing, or maybe it was about the curve of his chin. He wasn't all that good looking. Yes, he was nicely put together but it was something else. Maybe it was his bearing, the way he was talking to the people in his group in such a confident, easy way. He seemed so grounded. So solid.

Catherine gave herself an emotional shake. *Stop staring at him or you will make such a fool of yourself.* She decided to look in the other direction entirely and turned her back on him. It was a lovely late summer evening as the sun was setting over Edinburgh. She leaned out of the big open second floor window. The Festival was over and the tourists had departed which always made Catherine feel like she had her city back. The buzz was fine for a week or so until the volume of people cramming themselves into small spaces and bagging jimmy-hats by the dozen became cumbersome. No matter where Catherine had gone in the world, she always wanted to come back to live in Edinburgh – it was like the very land under her feet owned her. She belonged there and it felt like home.

Then, out of the corner of her eye she saw him walking over. He was coming directly towards her and she noticed her stomach constrict.

"Hello," he said with a warm Scottish accent.

Catherine wasn't certain if he was talking to her and froze. How cripplingly embarrassing it would be if she answered and he was talking to someone behind her. Better to just ignore him.

"That's some view!" he said as he stepped beside her at the window and sat down on the sill, indicating the sunset by toasting it with his drink. He turned then to look at her and smiled, a warm, lopsided, smile that put Catherine at ease.

She smiled back, unsure what to say.

"It is the most beautiful city in the world and I wouldnae bide onywhere else," he added, exaggerating his accent somewhat.

Catherine laughed and took a sip of her drink to avoid having to answer, but as the moment stretched on, she added with a shy smile and some heavy sarcasm, "It's alright I s'pose."

"Alright!? Have you seen that sunset? And the gorgeous silhouette of the New Town rooftops – it's stunning!" He grinned at her.

Although he was talking about the architecture, Catherine got the distinct impression that he was complimenting her, and she blushed a little. She smiled with appreciation when he offered to refill her wine glass.

Catherine soon found herself relaxing and chatting easily. Within half an hour the conversation had moved onto history and ghost stories of their city. Catherine began to tell him all about her experience at Tynemouth Priory and the unexplained and impossible memory she had uncovered.

"That was six years ago," Catherine raised her voice over the sound of the party music, "and it still bugs me. I know for a fact I was never there." Then with the sudden realisation that she'd been talking too much she clamped her mouth shut. This man was a stranger after all, someone she had only just met. Having had a couple of drinks she was already being far too open. Of course he wouldn't be interested in her mysterious random memory. He would think she was deranged.

To her surprise, and instead of running away, he looked thoughtful and curious. "Did you ask your folks? In case it was something that the family did and you'd simply forgotten?"

"Yeah, I got short shrift for that. My grandmother told me not to be ridiculous and of course I'd never been to Tynemouth. She asked if I was taking drugs!" Catherine still had to raise her voice above the music.

"What about your mum?"

"She was never in the picture." Catherine took a sip of wine and looked over her shoulder. It was not a subject she was ready to talk about. "I went back to Tynemouth, lots of times. Even lived there for a while. And I always experienced that same pull, the same fascination for the place. But I never remembered any more than I did that first time." She paused and, in that moment, Catherine noticed his clear blue eyes looking at her. Although the connection gave her a buzz she retreated and forced herself to look away. She mustn't look too keen. "What's your name anyway?"

He laughed and stuck out his hand, "Edward."

"Catherine." She swallowed hard as she shook his hand, feeling almost an electric shock of connection at the touch.

She had to admit that she found him quite attractive. His face was long and creased by laugh lines, whilst his blue eyes were full of mischief under his wavy light brown hair. He was the kind of man that she would have warned people to be wary of - confident, cocky and definitely a charmer.

They moved away from the window and got another glass of wine each whilst they chatted away about the weird and wonderful.

Then a tall blond girl burst through the crowd and grabbed Edward's arm. "Come and dance," she demanded.

Edward only had a moment to put down his glass and wink at Catherine before being dragged out. "Don't go away!" he said over his shoulder.

Catherine was intrigued and followed the couple into the other room. There Edward was already dancing with the girl amid a group of others. They made a beautiful couple. The blond was immaculately made-up, with her hair in a French plait and her short summer dress revealed a toned figure. He was holding her hand and spinning her right and then left, crossing and uncrossing their arms as they both spun to the rhythm. It was nothing like anything Catherine had ever seen before. Rather like a mix between rock'n'roll and 'Dirty Dancing'. She was fascinated and more than a little jealous.

When the music stopped Edward gave the girl a kiss on the cheek and then turned back towards Catherine, red-faced and breathing heavily.

"That looked amazing."

"It's called Ceroc. You should try it sometime!" Then he flashed a broad smile at her frightened look, and added with a laugh, "Don't worry I won't drag you onto the dancefloor."

"Was that your girlfriend?" Catherine tried to sound casual.

Edward almost spat out the water he was glugging down and laughed, "No, that's my sister, Fiona. That gives me an idea. Have you ever thought about hypnosis?"

"To help me dance?" Catherine laughed nervously.

"No, to help you find out about Tynemouth Priory? Maybe a hypnotist could help you find out what the connection is."

"Oh. I'd never thought of that," she was struck by the simplicity of the statement. Why had it never crossed her mind?

"Fiona knows someone who does regression hypnosis. He's really good at digging up subconscious memories. He takes them back to their childhood to discover why they have phobias. Helps them face their fears ... and stuff."

"Stuff?"

"Well, apparently quite a few of them regress back to previous lives – but I'm not sure whether I even believe in that kind of thing."

"Who do you know that he's helped?" She was intrigued but always cautious.

"Fiona has done it herself." He pointed across the room at the blond girl who was now looking very uncomfortable dancing with a man who had no sense of rhythm at all. Edward waved at her with an exaggerated cheery smile, and she gave him a filthy look back. "He cured her phobia of knives. She'd gotten so frightened over the years that she couldn't even eat with friends in case they waved a piece of cutlery at her." He waggled an imaginary knife in Catherine's direction.

"Wow, that must have been quite rough."

Fiona managed to escape from her dance partner and came over to join them. She took Edward's drink and ignored his pout. "What are you two talking about?"

"Hypnosis," said Edward. "I was telling Catherine here about your many phobias."

"Just the one!" Fiona nudged him hard with her elbow. "And hypnosis has helped." She smiled at Catherine, "It's opened my eyes to so many different things. Are you thinking about doing it?"

"It's a possibility, I have a random memory that I want explaining."

"Oh, I think it would definitely be worth trying then."

"Maybe I should give it a go," Catherine kept her face serene but inside was jumping cartwheels – how exciting that the mystery might be solved. Surely a hypnotist could help her understand who the other people were, and therefore why she'd been there. Or even help her discover more about how she travelled there. It was a small thing, a random memory but it had still bugged her as an unanswered question for six years.

Edward smiled and offered her another drink. The conversation moved on but before she left the party Catherine made sure that she got the name of the hypnotist from Fiona. In the taxi home she looked at the scrap of paper and smiled. She noticed, in a different handwriting, that Edward's name and number had been added as well.

Catherine looked up the hypnotist on her phone and made an appointment via his online booking system to see him. The man's name was Dr Sebastian Rayal. He had a very professional website, with testimonials from various happy customers which detailed how Dr Rayal had changed their lives through opening up their minds. She felt quite positive that he could help her remember more about her visit to Tynemouth, and maybe her mystery would be resolved. It was like a tiny itch that wanted scratching and she believed that even one session would give her the answers she needed.

~ 2 ~

Merwynn's Hall

Merwynn absently picked the meadow blossom and gazed at their gentle petals. The cheerful chirping of the birds proved there was no danger. Behind her stood the protective army of trees like warriors at her back – watchful, strong, safe. Her mother was there, smiling wistfully as she picked daisies and weaved them together into a crown with cowslip, meadow clary and a myriad of other blooms. Merwynn watched her with curiosity as the deft fingers knitted stem after stem into a thing of beauty, her heart swelling as she listened to her mother's familiar humming.

Her mother leaned forward with a little laugh and placed the circlet on Merwynn's red hair. In that action and sound Merwynn felt all the love and joy that her mother held for her, the solid security of knowing she meant something to someone. She mattered. Then Merwynn reached up and touched the fragile crown, already noticing the circle starting to fall apart.

"You're almost a woman now," her mother said in a remote voice and a tilt of the head. "So strong and wise, so much your own person."

Merwynn swallowed a lump in her throat. Something was wrong, but she couldn't put her finger on it. "Where have you been?" she frowned.

"Here," her mother answered, turning back to the flowers and picking more. "Always here."

Merwynn could feel herself fading, like something was slipping away. "Don't leave me again," she sobbed.

"I will never leave you," her mother took Merwynn's freckled face in her hand. Two sets of mirrored green eyes looking deep into each other. "I am always with you. I am yours and you are mine."

A blossom fell onto Merwynn's cheek as the flowers on her head fell apart. She reached up to catch them and in doing so woke herself up.

It was not a flower on her cheek but a tear. She wiped it away and sighed. It was a regular dream but each time she woke with the crushing weight of her grief again. She had spent nearly 11 years side by side with her mother learning to weave, spin, cook, and manage a household while her father was out supervising the tenants and managing their estate. Her mother had given birth to seven more children after Merwynn but the first three of them had not survived past infancy – leaving Merwynn and her mother alone for the first five years of her life. It was a precious time.

Her mother had smelt of wood smoke, and milk, and her broad smile brightened everything. Merwynn learnt to cook, to sew, to milk the cow, to churn butter and make cheese; she learnt how to plant the crops and tend the vegetables they ate. Mother and daughter worked alongside each other without instruction. At least that is how it seemed, though looking back, every touch of her hand was a lesson learnt. Together they had looked after new babies as they arrived with Merwynn helping to cuff her brothers when they misbehaved and showing her sister the ropes. Being the eldest she held a special place in her mother's heart, and to Merwynn, her mother was the world.

Then, one day, she was gone. She screamed and bled as she brought Merwynn's second sister into the world, and Merwynn was left holding the bloody, mewling babe as she watched her mother go quiet, and then she was no more.

At first Merwynn was numb. She couldn't comprehend a world in which her mother wasn't. However, she had been thrust into the role of lady of the house – not least with a newborn babe and three other children to care for. Sometimes her heart would ache and her stomach would clench when she thought of playing her mother's part. But now it was up to her to order everyone around and she didn't have a clue how to do it.

She reminded herself what her mother had taught her. "Open your eyes and your ears. Pay attention. Then speak as if the answer is obvious. People will follow you if they think you are sure."

So Merwynn faked it. She pretended to know what she was doing, and over time, she did.

For three summers she had kept house, taught her siblings their tasks whilst mothering the youngest and fighting to keep her alive. She clouted her brothers to milk the goats and fetch the water and pretended that everything was alright. During the day she used the grief fuelled anger to do her chores. At night though, she dreamed of her mother. They would talk and Merwynn would feel the warmth of her love again. She would bask in the comfort and the touch of her mother's arms. Only to once more awake to feel like a hole had been punched in the chest with her devastating loss.

Merwynn wiped the tear away. Better that her siblings did not see – they needed to know she was strong and could fill her mother's shoes and she didn't want to have to explain it away. Then she stretched out her limbs, pointed her toes and then bent her ankles, stretching tendon and sinew, feeling her muscles come to life before she started the day.

It was not yet light. So, slipping out from under the blankets and furs that she shared with her sisters, she set about rebuilding the fire. It was chilly and everyone would appreciate waking up to its warmth.

She sat on the edge of the firepit, stoking it with her mother's metal poker. This was her favourite part of the day. The quiet, uninterrupted moments before the work began. When men would have to be ushed from underfoot, and children bossed around to get their chores done. But for now, it was quiet and still.

She watched the shafts of sunlight start to filter through the roof, moving down the walls towards her. Once again, she would have to have words with her father, to have the thatch repaired before the rains set in. Then the warmth from the fire reached her bones and she smiled softly – patched though it was, this was home.

A cat sat regarding her from across the hall, fat from a night of feasting on mice. Merwynn's only companion during these early morning pockets of time. She reached out her hand to it and the creature approached sniffing at her fingers for any food. When none was forthcoming, he gave her a sideways glance but then allowed her to rub behind his ears before haughtily stalking off and curling up on her father's chair beside the fire.

Then she heard her brothers bickering and the peace was broken. She turned back to the cat, but he was nowhere to be seen. Time to start the day.

In the years to come Merwynn often looked back on that last morning. That last moment of family peace that she had. It was an oasis of calm for her, and the ending of her childhood.

"No." It was not an exclamation, just a flat denial. Merwynn gritted her teeth and once again, and more firmly, said, "No."

"Don't be ridiculous, girl, it was not a question. It is not your choice. It has been decided."

Merwynn looked her father straight in the eye, squared her shoulders and repeated, "No."

"You always were a stubborn girl, you will do what your father says."

Merwynn turned on the woman who was one of the many that warmed her father's bed since her mother died. "You have no right to interfere. Leave before I make sure you have a permanent reminder of that!" The threat was made more sinister by the quiet voice it was issued in and Merwynn felt triumphant when the woman clamped her jaw shut.

Merwynn's father showed signs of being too fond of his food. His long bristly hair and beard had already turned white, and he was rather too interested in his hawks and his women for Merwynn's liking. He was in other words, a typical thegn of the region. As far as Merwynn was concerned he was fat and lazy, and although he had once been into battle, she was sure that he would have remained at the back. He was nothing like her brave mother, who had fought against the marauding Gaels in the north before fleeing south and finding new places to settle north of the Humber river with her family.

"You WILL do as I say. I am your father. You will marry whom I tell you to."

Merwyn knew he was trying to sound confident, but he had never managed to command her to do anything. In fact, she viewed him with the same attitude as she ruled her younger brothers. Although she had never raised a hand to her father – after all, she knew the line that could not be crossed - nevertheless she had bossed him around the same.

Merwynn sighed and sat down on her mother's stool. She smoothed the folds of her dress over her knees as her father waited for an answer. With a casual air she replied, "I will not."

This was not the end of the fight but she also knew that nothing would compel her to marry the odious man her father had chosen for her. He was an old man, only a few years younger than her father. Oh, he was nice enough on the eye but he had a creepy nature that repulsed her. Hard rough hands which had pawed at her whenever she hadn't been able to escape from his clutches as a young girl. Her mother had often shooed him out of the hall and told Merwynn to stay clear of him. He had never forced himself upon her, but he had clearly decided that she was his from before she'd finished nursing. Whenever he visited her father's hall, he would pick her up onto his knee and cuddle her too close; stroke her cheek and her hair; kiss her neck and laugh when she tried to squirm out of his grasp. After her mother had died, he would leer at Merwynn and rub his crotch when they were alone. He had even told her of what delights he wished her to participate when they would be wed.

It would not happen. She could understand that her father wanted the alliance, and it would involve the family having more protection, but she would not be the bargaining chip. What could she do though? She was a high-born lady and it was her fate to be married off for her father's advantage. She could see her life planned out in front of her, and even if she managed to fend off this particular match, she would only be waiting around to be married off to someone else. A man that would hump her and put a baby in her belly. One that may well put her in her grave.

"I want to live, I want to be free to make my own choices," she spoke to no-one in particular - and so quietly that it sounded like a prayer.

Merwynn reached up and held the small ornate silver cross that hung on a leather thong around her neck. It had been her mother's and always felt like a connection to her. With a surge of hope, the idea came - the only way that her father could get a better match for her without losing face.

Her father was a pious man and her only alternative was to dedicate her life to the church. He had a good place in their community and would welcome that because it meant he had someone to pray for him and indeed he could promise the jilted groom prayers as well. Her father would even pay her required dowry to the church if she told him that she had been called to God. It was not a life she would choose for herself, but it was one that many would welcome. Her mother would have delighted in the idea of her being a nun.

Her throat tightened and she tried to blink back the prickling behind her eyes. No matter what happened she would be leaving her home. The place where she still sensed her mother around her, still felt the love that she had been gifted. She didn't want to go.

Her mother used to tell her stories about where she had come from. How as a child she had lived by the banks of the wide Foirthe river at the northern edge of the kingdom of Northumberland. They were attacked by an invasion force from the North. The Picts and the Gaels had united to fight off the marauding Vikings, and in turn had then sought to push across the Northumbrian border and take more of their northern lands. Her mother's village was overrun and burnt to the ground. The invaders saturated the area and the natives had to choose whether to be ruled or run. Merwynn's mother had come far south with her family and settled where the accursed Vikings had left many village huts and shelters empty and lands untilled. Here where her father's clan welcomed the refugees and helped them settle into a newer, albeit still dangerous, world. Her father had the saints watching over them though, someone who interceded with God to protect them. When the devils came, they would desert their homes and run to hide in the forests that covered so much of the land.

Those that didn't run or could not hide were killed or taken as slaves. It was a fact of life. The marauders would take what they wanted and move on and the locals would go back to their homes, grieve their losses and rebuild.

Over time, they had got very good at hiding their food stores and their silver, buried in caches which the Vikings rarely found. Her mother had told her about several such raids but they had not had an attack for as long as Merwynn had been alive.

Merwynn swallowed hard as she remembered how beautiful her mother was. How her long strawberry blond hair would fall across her face when she bent to cook flat scones over the hot stones by that very fire. She remembered how her mother would look up at her and smile, ruffling her messy red hair as she stood; how she would pick her up and swing her around; and then, for a rare moment, how her mother would sit beside her to look at the stitches she'd made in the cloth her daughter had sewed. Then she remembered how her mother had picked her up after a fall with two badly grazed knees. Merwynn had been pulling the dog's tail, and it had in turn chased her pushing her to the ground. Her mother had wiped her face, given her a hug, and said, "Don't cry, little one, that won't help at all. Your knees may sting for a little, but you have learnt a lesson for life!"

A movement caught Merwynn's eye and she looked up to see her youngest sister carrying a leather bucket of water past the open door. Her sister was nearly four summers old and was able to fend for herself, so she was now considered a full member of the family. Merwynn considered herself blessed and was proud that she had lost no more of her siblings in her mother's wake. At least she had succeeded there.

Being high born she also knew how to read and write. Her father had schooled her in the scriptures that he was so passionate about. He was a true believer and gave generous donations to the monks in return for prayers being said after his death. Her mother didn't need to pay for prayers as her daughter would pray for her, every day for the rest of her life.

Merwynn's mother had tried to teach her humility and self-sacrifice but, at that, she failed. As a wayward daughter, Merwynn knew she could not marry that man, could not bear the thought of him forcing himself on her without even the most tentative restraint. He would be like a rutting dog, tongue hanging out and panting his desire. The thought made her sick.

She got up and smoothed down the front of her dress. She knew her own mind. She would seek the protection of the church. She would become a nun.

~ 3 ~

Opening the Door

The day of Catherine's hypnosis appointment was dull and grey with a heaviness in the air which added to her apprehension. She wasn't at all sure about letting someone inside her conflicted head.

The hypnotist was based in George Street in central Edinburgh, and as Catherine hesitated outside the door, her hand hovering just above the door handle, she took a breath and opened it. She was struck by how professional it all looked inside – somehow, she had expected it to be seedy but it was like many other offices she had visited before. She waited in the plush reception area for her appointment and expected to be shown through by the receptionist but instead a well-dressed man came out to greet her.

"Hello, you must be Catherine," he said with an outstretched arm and, without waiting for a verbal response, shook her hand. He looked directly into her eyes and it made her feel rather uneasy, like a small animal caught in the eyeline of a hawk.

"Dr Rayal?"

"Call me Bastian, please," he said, still holding her hand in both of his.

He was an average-sized man, about five foot eight inches tall and looked relatively fit under his crew neck jumper and smart trousers; he had a goatee beard and cropped short dark wavy hair, both tinged with grey. It was his voice that made the biggest impression on her though. It had a warm quality which was very soothing, and she could see why Bastian had chosen the profession he had.

"Shall we?" he gestured politely, back towards the door he had come through.

Bastian's office was a picture of serenity – cream walls, and warm spot-lit ceiling, with little furniture and no clutter around. At one end of the room was a very tidy glass-topped desk with a modern looking computer and telephone, behind which sat a smart office chair and a metal filing cabinet to one side.

On the other side of the room was a comfy chair; a small glass coffee table holding a box of tissues, and a bottle of water with a glass. At right angles to the chair was an even more comfortable looking leather recliner. Soft music was playing almost like the trickling of water on the edge of her hearing and an aromatherapy candle made the place smell of wildflowers. Looking around Catherine could see pictures on the wall of serene country scenes - a sunlit forest, a flowery meadow and a calm sea vista. The whole room had a very mellow atmosphere.

Bastian gestured her towards the recliner, and she took a seat, now feeling a little awkward and unsure where to start. This was his domain, and she felt a bit out of her depth, but resisted the urge to chew on a finger nail.

Bastian settled into his chair and folded his hands in his lap as he regarded her. Once in the room he remained silent waiting for her to speak and the seconds ticked by without comment.

"So … how do we start?" Catherine was unable to think of anything else to say.

"That's up to you," he paused, "tell me what's brought you here?"

She took a deep breath and started to tell the story about her isolated memory of Tynemouth Priory; about how she didn't understand why she could remember somewhere she had never been and wanted to know more.

"I don't know why it bothers me so much, but it is so odd. I have a really good memory – in fact it is something that I am quite proud of. But this is worse than forgetting something, this is remembering something that never happened." Catherine looked Bastian straight in the eye, she wanted to make sure he understood that she was sane and in full control of her faculties. "Can you help me? I mean, to recognise the people I was with, or to see how I got there, or even why we were there in the first place? Even to know who the other girl was?" Catherine noticed the blood rushing to her cheeks, she felt foolish asking for the impossible. What right did she have to take up other people's time with this nonsense.

Bastian nodded and looked intrigued, his expressive eyebrows raised, "I'm sure I can help," he said with an air of confidence. "What do you know of hypnosis already?"

"Just a layman's understanding that it's tapping into the subconscious." She paused, but Bastian seemed to be waiting for her to say more. His eyes bored into her like drills, compelling her to talk, even though she didn't have anything else to add. "To be honest I haven't thought about it before and don't have a clue other than the media hype I've seen."

"Every day, or rather every night, you go into the deepest of hypnotic trances. A trance in which your surroundings, even your everyday world, is forgotten. A state of mind in which you can do anything, from flying through the air to being the Queen of Sheba."

"You're talking about dreaming?" Catherine was pleased with herself that she had cottoned on to what he was referring to.

"Yes. We all spend around 25% of our sleep time in REM state or 'dreaming' if you prefer - whether you recall those dreams later or not. When you go under hypnosis, you're basically entering the REM state whilst still awake. So unlike dreaming you are still awake and aware of your surrounding. This may sound like an odd question, but do you read books?"

"Yes, I read quite a lot." Truth be told, books had been Catherine's only friends growing up – they took her into imaginary worlds and in their pages, she could be anyone. She could be popular, interesting and attractive – the pages didn't care if she was small, or weak, or a burden. They kept her from being underfoot, and always welcomed her in.

"Good, then you will know how it feels when you're reading a good book, and how you get lost in the story. You are still aware that you are sitting in a chair with paper and ink in your hands. Your eyes are interpreting the words on the page: but your mind and consciousness are elsewhere – immersed in the story you are reading, surrounded by those characters and that architecture."

Catherine nodded – she recognised the felling when she had a book in her hands – it was something she could easily be lost in, and often was.

"But you are still present and able to respond to the real world - for example if the phone rings you are instantaneously back in the day-to-day world. That is very similar to hypnosis except we are reading your subconscious instead of a book. It's my job to help you get to the subconscious state by relaxation and keep you there whilst you experience what you need to. So we can tap into any subliminal thoughts and memories."

Catherine laughed nervously. "What if my subconscious is a horror story and wants to kill me? What if I don't wake up again, or do something embarrassing?" She tried to make light of it but deep down she was scared of what she might find out.

What if this stranger was to discover she had nothing worthy underneath the surface at all.

She had hoped that Bastian would laugh too and it might break the tension. He didn't seem to find it amusing though leaned back in his chair as his tone changed to one similar to a teacher she remembered from primary school.

"The subconscious state is a safe place. Our brains have to go through it to get to the *deeper sleep state* and go through it again to also wake up to the *alert state* every morning. It's where much of your hidden potential lies and where the subconscious mind is dominant."

"That makes sense," Catherine nodded, trying to sound like she had got it, but was still struggling to take it all in. Asking more questions might make her look stupid so she decided to take him at his word.

He had a half smile on his face – it was clear he had seen through her blasé response and continued to explain. "It's where your experiences and emotions and deep-rooted memories can be accessed. It's a perfectly normal and natural place that everyone visits multiple times every day. Drivers going on a familiar route often have no memory of the journey when they arrive at their destination. They were in control of the car at all times though and should anything have happened would have been able to snap back into action. The mind is in two different places at once – one place is relaxed and experiences new things whilst the other is still in control. Tell me do you have any concerns or worries about the process?"

"Just that I am not sure about being under someone else's control." Did she really admit that?

"I cannot control my clients nor what happens, that is all you. No-one can be hypnotised against their will, nor can they be hypnotised to do something against their nature."

"I didn't know that." Catherine felt a small boost now they were talking about people in general instead of specifically focusing on her.

Bastian leaned forward, elbows on his knees and hands clasped in front of him, "As children, we have a literal open mind, we absorb everything like sponges, and store it all away in massive subconscious data banks. But as we grow up our minds become more analytical and critical, stopping us from accessing that data. During sleep our critical minds switch off leaving us open to suggestion and able to resolve issues we might analytically think have no solutions – it also shows us snippets of those subconscious thoughts but with no means to analyse them. A hypnotic state is much more child-like and the patient will accept suggestions which they might not when their critical mind is switched on – allowing people to face their fears, beat their addictions, and bring clarity to memory."

"Wow. That sounds pretty amazing, I had never thought of it that way before." Maybe this wouldn't be so bad – and it would be good to have some answers.

"Not many people do, there is such an image of the famous media hypnotists working their magic on stage – clicking their fingers and someone goes under. Did you know that's not possible? You're not allowed to show the process of hypnosis on television – because you might hypnotise the people watching at home. The volunteers are taken aside before the show starts and put under with a suggestion - with the consent of the volunteer - that when in front of the TV audience they will go back under when the hypnotist clicks their fingers and says *Sleep*." Bastian demonstrated by clicking his fingers as he said the word.

"Really!?" Catherine laughed at how brazen it was.

"Yes," Bastian was laughing too now. "So they are already under hypnosis when the supposedly volunteer from the show itself. It is a bit of a cheat but it seems to be the only way it can be done. Plus it ensures that the hypnotist doesn't pick someone that refuses to go under."

"Good point," she grinned, "that could be problematic." She felt relief when Bastian laughed, like a moment of connection and it put Catherine more at ease.

Bastian sat back in his chair again looking satisfied, "So," he said, "shall we see what we can find out?"

Catherine nodded.

"I think the key might be the other girl you remember – maybe we could try and go back to access memories of her? Putting the relationship with her in context might help you understand why you were there?"

"Okay," she said, now feeling less apprehensive. Bastian knew what he was talking about. She had no idea whether or not it would work as she had never tried before, but Bastian seemed the right person to try with.

"Just sit back into the chair, make sure you feel relaxed."

She lay back on the recliner, which produced a footrest when pushed back. It was comfortable with her arms supported on the cushioned armrests. It was almost like she was floating. Bastian turned up the soothing music with the noise of running water mirroring the hesitant rain that had started falling outside again. Then he began to talk her into a relaxation state.

His voice was deep, slow and clear. "Take a deep breath in, and then exhale. I am going to get you to relax further. Let your mind go blank, feel yourself getting heavier and sinking into the chair. Now close your eyes."

The chair hugged her and she felt at ease, so she let his voice wash over her and her mind distance itself from her body.

"Feel your toes relaxing and all the tension evaporating from them. You can feel a warmth as the muscles release and each part of your body relaxes further. Feel that warmth rising up through the arch of your feet, and into your heels. Then feel your ankles relax and your calves, the back of your knees sinking further into the chair. Feel your thighs and hips relax melting all the tension away ..."

It surprised her how much his voice soothed her, Catherine's legs were already much heavier and relaxed than she thought possible. As he continued to talk, she started to sink into the recliner as all the tension dissipated in her shoulders, arms and neck. By the time he reached her head she was already drifting.

"Now I want you to imagine a cleansing light coming into you through your head. Let it travel through your whole body all the way through to your toes and out again."

She found that she could almost see the light and encouraged it to flood over and through her.

Before her were a set of stairs, a long flight going downwards which she started to descend. Step, by step, she went, and with each stair she felt more relaxed, and became more aware of the place she was in. It was warm and safe and she was in no hurry. Everything, other than the steps, slipped away – no walls or ceiling, and although she was aware of a handrail to support her, she didn't need to use it.

At the bottom of the stairs was a door which she knew would lead her where she needed to go. She opened it.

"Where are you?" said the voice.

"I'm in a room. A small room."

The cell can only have been about eight feet long by six feet wide; it had an unglazed window with open shutters and a thick heavy curtain pulled across to one side; opposite the window was a wooden door, ajar. A small simple wooden wardrobe stood by the door and against the wall was a stone pallet topped by a straw filled mattress and a thick woollen blanket.

This was not her sleeping quarters.

She looked down at herself, confused to be there. She was wearing odd garments: a long brown coloured tunic-like top which reached half-way down her thighs, over a rough off-white shirt laced at the wrists; some sort of thick hose which were secured with cord around her waist and leather shoes which were tied up to her ankles. The tunic had simple embroidery on it but no collar; it was also loosely tied in at the waist with a leather belt – the buckle of which was a battered circular Celtic design of a snake swallowing its tail. Over her shoulders she had pulled on a long black hooded woollen cloak secured across the chest with two circular pins joined by a short chain.

"What are you doing?"

"I'm dressing. I am hurrying to get away."

She was aware of the urgency. Through the open window she could see the sea and the waves were crashing on the shore. The silver sands of the small bay were bathed in the bright moonlight as it awaited the turning of the tide. She had to get away.

With a jolt of terror something caught her attention. Through the window it appeared that a dense black cloud surged up from the sea. She felt as if a something was pushing its way through the air and into the room - pulling her towards the window like a vacuum.

"NO!" she shrieked.

"What's happening?"

"There is something coming. Something terrifying."

"Can you get away?"

She looked over her shoulder at the door, pulling away from the dark force that was trying to engulf her. "I don't know." She dragged a foot backwards away from the darkness, the pull lessened and she felt a surge of hope. Another step and then with a wrench she was free from the grip of terror. Without a moment's thought she pulled the door open, scraping it as it dragged across the stone floor.

"I'm out of the room."

"Where are you now?"

"I'm in some sort of dark hallway." The dim tunnel led away from the room, she ran the fifteen feet to the corner and then up the stairs which were there. On the top step was another door which she knew led out into the air again – she pulled it open and went through. She was in front of the priory gatehouse between the walls and the dry moat. The air was clean, and she could breathe, but something was deeply wrong.

Catherine screamed.

"Are you alright?" Bastian asked.

"Yes," she was rather shaken and found she was breathing hard. She put a hand to her chest and willed herself to calm down. She could feel her heart pounding under her palm.

"You were getting distressed, so I thought it better to bring you out of it. Do you know how long you were under?"

"A few minutes," she answered, finding the question odd.

"No, you have been under hypnosis for over an hour. Look at the clock." He pointed at the glazed timepiece on the wall and she instinctively looked up. An hour and ten minutes had passed since she had started to relax in the recliner. She was stunned.

"Time passes differently when you are under hypnosis," he said. How do you feel about what just happened?" Bastian asked.

"Confused." She told him about the room she had run from and how she knew Tynemouth well – but there was no tower or building on that side of the rock. "There is only a cliff and beach. There's a wall but that's all. Does that mean it is all in my head?"

"I don't know," he said. "Does it matter? It's obviously something that you need to work through. I think this may go deeper than you anticipated."

She nodded, and he continued. His confidence and calm manner made her feel a little better, but she could still feel her heart beating fast.

"How does this relate to my memory, when I was in Tynemouth as a teenager though? It doesn't make any sense to me."

"Sometimes past lives can come into present lives,' he said, speaking slowly. He thought for a moment before continuing. 'Maybe the girl you saw as a teenager wasn't really there but showing you around a place you had been before. Maybe she was you in a past life? Memory can play tricks. The most important thing is to move forward and explore this further. Your subconscious is definitely trying to tell you something." Bastian paused for a moment as he watched her closely. "I would suggest we meet again soon. Does next Thursday work for you?"

"I think so," she was still reeling from the experience. She didn't feel quite ready to move but it was clear from Bastian's body language that the session was over. She struggled out of the chair's embrace and got to her feet – still feeling rather dreamy and distant.

She shook Bastian's hand and again which helped her feel more grounded again – remarkable how she had come to feel safe with him. He had very intense eyes which never left her whilst they were talking, plus his lack of scepticism was very reassuring. However, as she left his office, she was frustrated with herself. She had expected an answer to her original mystery, not another riddle to solve, and although the experience had felt extremely real – in fact it was more like a memory than a dream – she was not sure she believed it. The place she had seen under her hypnosis didn't exist, and as far as she had seen from several visits to Tynemouth over the years, had never existed.

She walked along George Street, pulling her coat up around her neck, and feeling rather detached. In an absent-minded dash she escaped the increasingly heavy rain by ducking into a book shop; then started to wander around the aisles on automatic pilot. Catherine had always found book shops soothing places, being surrounded by wisdom, humour, insights and history made her feel more in perspective within her own life. She loved the smell of the books; as well as watching people focusing on different worlds and ideas as they leafed through the pages of other people's musings.

It was whilst she was absorbed in the atmosphere of the shop that she noticed someone calling her name for a second time. She looked around and didn't recognise the man coming towards her.

Then Catherine's brain made the connection and she smiled with genuine pleasure. "Hello Edward."

~ 4 ~

Monastic Life

Life in the monastery was good although Merwynn missed her siblings, her friends, and even the cats. She left her old life behind when she had persuaded her father to allow her to join the nuns of St Hilda at the abbey in Hackness. However, it was an all-female community of kind and hard-working souls, and Merwynn was happy there. St Hilda herself had founded the abbey at Hackness the same year that she died, over a century before, and as patron saint they knew that she watched over the band of women like a proud mother.

Each day was filled to bursting as the abbey housed travellers, nursed the sick and assisted the poor. The nuns observed numerous services of daily prayer - on rising, at the lighting of the evening lamp, at bedtime and at midnight. They would also pray at the third, sixth, and ninth hours of the day as well as listen to scripture during mealtimes.

Merwynn dutifully joined in with all the prayers but often found her mind wandering and developed the talent of dozing whilst on her knees in prayer. This did occasionally invite a painful nudge in her ribs from an older nun to her side, especially during Matins in the middle of the night. However, Merwynn detected a hint of a smile on the nun's face even through the prescribed scowl at her disrespect. Indeed no matter how often it happened the older nun never told on her.

Merwynn had her chores of tending the communal monastic gardens which provided medicines and food for the nuns and the local community. She liked being outside and the chores were not overly hard. Along with her fellow nuns she also tended the orchards, the fishponds and dovecots. On top of all this, Merwynn took time out of every day to teach the local noble children the scripture stories – in Latin of course.

Merwynn enjoyed being close to children again. The children were used to harsh reprimands if they misbehaved and, in Merwynn's opinion, some of the nuns were a little too quick to lash out. Many a time one or other of the children had run to her and cuddled in close to her after receiving a scolding.

In her lessons Merwynn tried to make sure the children enjoyed the time. She would tell stories from the scriptures, getting the children to sit around her feet – like her mother had done with her. Sometimes if one of them had tried extra hard with reciting the psalms she would let them sit on her lap whilst she told the story.

One little girl – Cwen – always tried to get the prized placement on Merwynn's lap. She was a pretty little girl, the daughter of the local lord, always cheerful and bright, quick to laugh with bright blue eyes that followed Merwynn everywhere she went. It made Merwynn smile to see Cwen chew her little red lip as she strained to remember the Latin phrases. The blond curls being twisted around her small fingers as she tried to get her lips and tongue around the words. Cwen reminded Merwynn of herself as a young girl, vying for her mother's attention, and it made her feel good to be seen as such a treasure to the children in her care.

Sometimes, as long as Merwynn knew that none of the other nuns could overhear, she would tell the children tales that were not of a religious nature. She would share stories that she'd been told of her mother's clan – the bravery of their flight from danger and how they left everything behind to find a better future. It made Merwynn's heart sore to see the rapt attention of the children and the awe at the heroism of her mother and her family. She knew it was a sin of pride but talking about her mother in some ways kept her alive for Merwynn.

She talked to the children about what to do if they ever found themselves attacked. To run, find somewhere to hide, and to stay quiet until the danger had passed. To the children though, the attacks were remote and a long time in the past – to their young, bright and open minds the Vikings were figments of the adults' imaginations and they could not fathom it ever happening to them. Still Merwynn assured them – the danger was always present and they should heed their elders.

Merwynn felt that she was giving something back and making her mother proud to help mould and shape these young people. So, all in all, being a nun was a fulfilling life, and she was content with her lot.

Merwynn had only been at Hackness a year or two when a messenger arrived to announce that the father of twin girls in Merwynn's care had been killed. Merwynn and another older nun were tasked by the Abbess to travel by cart with the distressed girls back to their home near the coast. Merwynn was to console them on the journey and ensure that they arrived safely whilst the older nun drove the cart. Their mother would be hurriedly gathering their things so as to vacate the hall before her husband's brothers came to claim it, and possibly her and her daughters as well.

On the way, Merwynn told them stories of St Hilda. How Hilda had been a pagan and was baptised when she was a few years older than them. It was not serving as a distraction though so Merwynn started to tell them instead about how St Hilda had rid the area of a plague of snakes. Firstly, Hilda had prayed to God to turn the snakes to stone but then a young nun had said that the snakes could still bite you with stone fangs. So, St Hilda prayed that God would also remove their heads.

Since then people had been finding the snakes all over the area, headless, coiled and turned to stone. If only the girls could find one of these snakes it would prove to them that St Hilda was blessed, and that their father was indeed on his way to heaven. That they would see him again once their mortal days were done.

The girls were delighted, they had three of these stone snakes depicted on their father's coat of arms. Merwynn gasped outwardly with surprise, but inside she smiled as it was something that she already knew. The girls then also said they had seen many of these headless stone snakes on the beaches around their home and had many more decorating their hall. Merwynn was genuinely surprised by this as she had always thought the story a charming old wife's tale.

When the cart arrived at the twin's coastal hall, Merwynn saw the sea for the first time. It took her breath away. She had never seen anything so huge in her life, and it undulated with a power which overwhelmed her with awe. Here was the power of God, here was something that she could touch and see. This was what she felt could be worshipped. Leaving the twins with their mother she begged leave to visit the shore and walked down to the water's edge. The feeling was immense, the connection undeniable. Merwynn had to remove her leather shoes and lift her skirts as she stood ankle deep in the water. It was intoxicating, and delightful.

Before she left for the cart ride home, the twins came up to her, pulling their mother along with them. The mother looked both tired and pale but held her head high in her grief. Merwynn noticed that she carried something in her hands as she approached.

Merwynn hugged both the girls and wished them well and hoped to one day see them again. The girls hugged her back and said they had a gift for her. Their mother then handed Merwynn a coiled stone snake about the width of her hand. It was small but heavy and at first, Merwynn wanted to drop it, feeling that it might somehow come alive. Then she looked at it more closely. The snake had most certainly been turned to stone and its head had been removed – just like the legend said. It was an amazing thing.

"Thank you for your kindness," said the mother as she put an arm around each of her daughters. "I hope this small token will remind you of us."

Merwynn thanked the mother for the thoughtful gift and wished them all luck, and as the cart set off back towards the monastery at Hackness she tucked the stone snake safely in her pocket. She talked all the way home with the other nun about other stories and miracles that St Hilda was famous for. For the first time in her life, Merwynn started to believe in something bigger than herself. She started to believe in St Hilda, that in her protection and, in God's grace, maybe life would remain as it was. Safe, secure, kind, and happy. The days might be long, and the work hard, but as far as Merwynn was concerned, she was giddy with life, and everything was right with the world.

~ 5 ~

Not An Option

"Hi Catherine, how lovely to see you. What are you doing here?" Edward flashed a straight row of white teeth as he smiled. It was infectious and made her naturally smile back.

"Just browsing."

"Got time for a coffee?" he asked indicating with his folded newspaper the plush coffee area in the shop.

"Sure," she was quite relieved to be pulled back into the present day. Although she'd only met Edward once before, she found his natural enthusiasm endearing. He was rather good company. She still had his phone number in the pocket of her jacket but had never for a moment considered calling him. She doubted very much that he was interested and was rather surprised that he even remembered her name.

They talked about mundane stuff to do with ordering coffee and the girl serving behind the counter smiled warmly as he placed the order. It looked like he was a regular there. Catherine was comfortably surrounded by the modern sounds of the coffee shop. The steam, the gentle clinks of cups being moved around, and the bangs as the barista emptied the previous coffee grounds from the machine. It was all very familiar and safe as she inhaled the nutty fragrances.

As they sat down Catherine noticed the headline on Edward's newspaper. A politician had committed suicide rather than face the ongoing investigation into his illicit affair.

"Brings a whole new meaning to political suicide huh?" Edward quipped.

"I can't think of anything more selfish," Catherine replied with a sharper tone than she had meant to, as she glanced at the story.

"Really?"

"Ok, so he was in trouble, but rather than face the music he took the coward's way out. I had a friend at Uni whose dad committed suicide. Such a waste. Left her mum with four kids to bring up and no insurance or any support of any kind. It devastated the family. My friend was really messed up because of it."

A momentary awkward silence ensued. Edward opened his mouth and closed it again, then changed the subject. "So, what have you been up to since I last saw you? Did you go see that hypnotist?"

"Yes, as a matter of fact, I've just come from there."

"How did it go?"

"I am not sure. I expected him to be able to resolve the issue but instead he regressed me back to a past life... or something." Catherine trailed off, unable to properly articulate what had happened and once again feeling like she had said too much.

"That sounds exciting."

She had been expecting him to laugh at her but he looked genuinely interested. "It could be my over-active imagination," she laughed at herself instead.

"Did it feel like your imagination?"

Slightly embarrassed by her flippancy and annoyed with herself that she had dismissed her own experience, her façade finally dropped away. "Honestly, no, it all seemed so real.

Strangely more real than this is right here and now. Like that's waking and this is the dream."

"Were you Cleopatra or something?" he said, some of his usual teasing humour returning.

"No," she pretended to cuff him. "I was a girl dressed as a man in some medieval garb – weird kind of leg garments attached at the waist with a belt. I was at Tynemouth Priory I know that. Then something happened, something was coming for me and I ran away. I screamed when he brought me out of it."

"Wow, sounds pretty dramatic. I know that Fiona found the whole experience life changing. She wouldn't talk to me about it though – I guess she thought I would tease her."

"Would you have?"

He laughed again, "Yes, I suppose I would."

"For all your teasing, you seem quite close."

"Yes, we are. Now at least."

Catherine detected a note of sadness in his voice, she didn't want to make him uncomfortable so redirected the conversation. "I would have loved to have had a sibling growing up but it wasn't to be. My grandmother always used to say *One child is MORE than enough trouble.*"

"She sounds a delight!" he said with a sarcastic tone, brightening a little.

Catherine got the distinct feeling that he was grateful she had changed the subject. "She was okay – very strict and very keen for me to do well in my studies. She made me work and that is no bad thing."

"So, you were an only child?" Edward was smiling.

"Yes, and no."

"Oh?"

"My mum… well she was quite young when she had me. She never showed any interest… left it to my grandmother to raise me. Mum was a nurse and married the first doctor she could hook her claws into. Apparently, I have a couple of half-brothers but I've never met them. I haven't seen her for years." Catherine swallowed down the now familiar lump that arose every time she had told people about her mum. She wanted to be honest – that indeed she had a bed of thorns where the warmth of a loving family should be - but talking about it always threatened to overwhelm her. She knew that nothing could be done about it but endure and she couldn't bear the pity looks if she showed her emotions about the subject. "I'm very lucky that my grandparents were there for me."

"Sounds tough," Edward said looking directly into her eyes.

Catherine held his eyes for a heartbeat and then looked away, picking up her spoon and stirring her already perfectly mixed coffee. "No, not at all. It was mostly just my gran and me. My grandfather was never around much, more interested in his golf magazines. My grandmother was super strict but she was a good teacher, made sure I read books rather than watched TV, taught me how to clean up after myself, and made me study hard. She prepared me for the world outside. She wasn't touchy-feely but she did her best by me."

Catherine took another sip of coffee, deliberately avoiding his gaze, she didn't want to see any judgement or sympathy there. Any reaction was uncomfortable and so she stared at her cup as she continued to stir. She couldn't bear the silence for long though so tried to think of something to ask him. "What do you do for a living anyway Edward?"

"I work in IT – training people on computers and how to design websites. Pretty boring stuff but it's what I know. The only thing I really love about it is keeping up with technology – my company sends me on loads of courses to keep ahead of the competition."

"So, you're a bit of a learning junkie then?"

"Yeah, you could say that."

He was smiling in that slightly squint way again and Catherine couldn't tell why she found it so attractive. Was it the cheekiness about it or revealing a boyish charm? Whatever it was, Catherine felt lightheaded as she looked into his eyes.

Then she jumped up as if stung by a bee, at the same time reddening with embarrassment. "Shit shit shit!" She was supposed to be at work; she had taken the morning off for the hypnosis session but was due back before now. Although she didn't have any afternoon appointments, she was sure that her boss would have noticed and been frowning at her empty desk. "I'm late for work! Sorry – I have to run."

He looked downcast that she was going. "How about we go out for an evening sometime next week then?" he said.

"Okay," she scribbled her mobile number on a napkin as she grabbed her coat and said, "give me a call."

She could hear Edward laughing at her discomfort as she dashed out of the door back into the rain. She felt gawky and awful at running away from him like that but at the same time rather overwhelmed by the whole meeting. He seemed very nice, attractive, funny and intelligent - there had to be a flaw somewhere. There was no chance he would be attracted to someone like her.

Back at the office Catherine sat staring blankly at the spreadsheet full of data points on her computer screen, the numbers blurring together. She couldn't focus. The hypnosis session with Dr Rayal kept replaying in her mind.

It had felt so real - the scratchy wool tunic, the cold sea air, the impending sense of doom. But it couldn't be an actual memory. She must have conjured up those vivid images from her overactive imagination.

Catherine minimised the spreadsheet and pulled up a search browser, typing in *past life regression hypnosis*. Maybe this was some sort of syndrome that created false memories. Knowledge would help her make sense of this strangeness.

She became absorbed in reading the research, clinical trials, and sceptical examinations of recovered memory therapy. The science was conflicting, inconclusive. Some argued it could uncover buried trauma, others that it caused false memories.

Catherine sighed, removed her reading glasses and massaged her temples. She had work to do, not personal internet searches. As a research analyst for a pharmaceutical company, her job was to compile data and identify statistical trends, not delve into fringe psychology.

Returning to the spreadsheet, she toggled to the next tab of data. Her team was assessing the efficacy of a new cancer drug, crunching the numbers from trial studies and quantifying treatment outcomes. It was crucial research, even if tediously detail-oriented at times.

Catherine's mind wandered again to the dank stone cell and the feeling of being terrified and trapped. She shook her head. Focus. She couldn't fall behind. She was lucky to have this job, and able to apply her science background. If she kept performing well, a promotion to lead researcher was likely.

She resumed meticulously auditing the data, checking and double-checking. Catherine took comfort in the orderly columns of figures. Here, in the realm of facts and observable outcomes, she was in control. Everything could be defined, measured, and analysed. Not like the chaos of emotions and hallucinations creeping in from her past. She needed to keep those irrational thoughts at bay, locked up tight. Sticking to logic and reason had gotten her this far in life. She had to believe it could keep carrying her forward too.

~ 6 ~

Haystack

Merwynn was working in the physic garden mid-morning after a light rain had done all her watering for her. She was humming and enjoying the freshness of the air, and the smell of the herbs as she pottered amongst the medicinal plants.

That was when she heard a short scream.

Her stomach constricted as she instinctively put her hand in her pocket gripping St Hilda's snake in her fist. Since her trip to the coast, she had taken to carrying the snake with her everywhere, as a talisman, and finding its weight in her pocket reassuring. She froze to listen. For a few breathless heartbeats she could hear nothing, like the whole world was still. Even the bees seemed to have stopped their incessant search for nectar. Merwynn hoped that one of the nuns had simply tripped and fallen, and as the silence stretched on, she started to feel that was all it was.

Now unfrozen, she moved toward the sound to see if help was needed. Then a bell started to ring frantically. It was cut short with another scream. A cacophony erupted with the battle cry of men roaring as they charged.

With a horror she felt in her bowels, Merwynn knew they were being attacked. She was dizzy and it was difficult to breathe. Vikings. The very word held terror for all. The screams came from everywhere. Merwynn's heart pounded in her chest and her breath came in short bursts.

Inside the walls of the monastery, they were trapped – unable to run to a forest to escape. The walls that were supposed to keep them safe had ensnared them for slaughter.

Her instinct to hide had taken over, so she suppressed her urge to scream. Merwynn ran to the wall and put her back to it. She slunk into the shadows moving carefully away from the exposed gardens. Wide eyed and holding her breath, she peaked around the garden wall to see that the Vikings were busy searching the buildings, dragging the nuns into the courtyard and turning over barrels and boxes. The noise was everywhere – screaming and shrieking of women; the roaring of men; the scraping of swords, the clang of metal hitting stone, and the sickening sounds of death. The brutes were swarming over the whole complex.

The smell of fear was everywhere, the metallic tang of blood mingled with the acrid urine of terror. Merwynn clutched St Hilda's snake tighter and prayed for deliverance, then she girded her courage and dashed behind a group of men into the back of the kitchens. She hid behind a wooden pillar as a dishevelled half-dressed, terrified nun ran in the other door. A large leather-clad huge brute of a Viking chased in after, his crooked and dented helm still upon his head. He grabbed the girl by her loosen hair with a force that pulled her off her feet. Merwynn pushed back into the shadows and stood as still as she could as he threw the young nun onto the table and pulled up her torn robes. Merwynn wanted to look away but terror rooted her to the spot. The girl screamed and thrashed about scratching her attacker's neck. He roared, punching the girl in the face. She instantly went limp, then he continued to assault her as blood poured from her smashed eye and cheek. Merwynn's stomach lurched and she swallowed hard to stop herself from vomiting. Quietly, and ever so carefully, she crept her way behind them; step by terrified step towards the door, her lips prised together, and keeping as close to the wall as she could. Feeling both grateful and sickened that the attacker's attention was otherwise occupied.

As soon as she was through the door, she picked up her skirts and made for the main gates but hid behind a barrel at the corner of the barn when she saw a band of the daemons in the courtyard. She could not see any way out. The beasts had surrounded a number of whimpering and crying nuns who were tied together with rope. Merwynn desperately looked one way and then the other. Panic threatened to overwhelm her as a long-haired blond brute started to walk in her direction. Her heart was hammering and every nerve was on high alert. Eyes taking in every detail of the men who were attacking them. The flecks of spittle on their beards, their huge hands, the gleam of their axes and swords, and the dark blood on their alien clothes.

There were only moments before the blond brute would get close enough to see her and she would be lost. Merwynn glanced around the other side of the barrel at the group of women – they at least were still alive. Her eyes met with those of the older nun who had travelled to the coast with her only those few weeks before. Without hesitation the woman stood up and started yelling at the invaders.

The blond Viking changed direction, turning back to the group he pulled the older nun to her feet and calmly skewered her on his sword. She had a look of surprise on her face as she stared at her killer, then she collapsed in a heap at his feet. Blood and excrement leaked from her. He kicked her dead body and then spat on her. The other nuns went silent.

Merwynn used the momentary distraction to duck inside the barn. Her last chance of a hiding place. The smell of the dung in the stack of used hay caught her nostrils. A chance, somewhere that no-one would want to hide. She clawed her way through the damp straw, gagging on the fumes. Right under into the centre of the pile.

When deep enough into the pile she touched something warm and alive. It flinched. It was the child Cwen – shivering and wild eyed with terror. They had both jumped when Merwynn touched her but Cwen relaxed when she recognised her teacher and seemed comforted by Merwynn's presence. She shifted over to let Merwynn get further under the hay and in that instant, they heard the wooden barn door being kicked aside. They both froze, eyes locked on each other and breath caught.

Moments of silence stretched out as Merwynn strained to listen for any tiny sound. Had he seen her entering the barn? Did he know they were there? Or was he just searching randomly?

Cwen stiffened, then screamed and started to thrash around as she started to move rapidly backwards. She clawed at the ground trying to get away as she was pulled out of the hay. Cwen cried for help and reached out to grab Merwynn's hands but, with her heart shattering, Merwynn pulled her arms away and under her chest. Tears poured from Merwynn's eyes. She was powerless to help the child, she knew that, but it still cut her to the quick. It was hopeless. They would both be doomed if Merwynn tried to hold onto her – or even made a sound. Cwen was dragged out of the haystack, kicking and screaming. Then Merwynn listened with horror as her screams got further away and was sickened by her own relief that the brute was not searching further.

Merwynn lay in that haystack crying bitter silent tears for hours, her hand clamped over her mouth trying to hold back the sobs and shivering for fear of giving herself away. The screams, the callous laughter and the guttural male voices ebbed and flowed through the day and into the night. Finally the emotional and physical exhaustion took their toll and

Merwynn fell into unconsciousness. The memory of Cwen's eyes pleading and her hands reaching out clawed at her heart and haunted her dreams.

She awoke with a start to silence. The sound of the Vikings had disappeared, and the smell of smoke and death mixed with the stale hay. Stunned and broken, Merwynn prayed for half a day more, clutching the stone snake tightly in one hand and her silver cross in the other, every nerve on alert for the slightest noise. Eventually, hunger and thirst drove her out of her hiding place.

Only a handful of the nuns had survived the attack, most having been assaulted or beaten and left for dead. Merwynn alone had come out without any visible injury.

The Vikings had taken anything of value and all the harvested food. They had destroyed everything else. A couple of the buildings were still smouldering, but the Vikings had only made a half-hearted attempt to set fire to them. Having got what they came for – a small amount of silver, slaves, and food – they must have been in a hurry to leave.

For hours Merwynn wandered through the buildings and the gardens searching in vain for Cwen, praying that she had somehow escaped the men and was hiding in fear.

Each time she came across another dead friend her heart broke a little bit more as she wept and knelt to pray over the body. Another piece of her died with each of them. Then she helped the others drag the carcasses back to the half-ruined church.

As the others tried to rest, Merwynn continued searching in every possible place for Cwen, over and over again, until one of the other nuns grabbed her arm.

"Come away Merwynn, she's gone."

"She can't be," Merwynn sobbed as she was flooded with memories of children running through the compound. Their voices raised in laughter as they played some game or other.

Whilst their joy had made Merwynn smile, she was haunted by echoes of her own voice telling them to be quiet. She should have told them to relish every moment.

"Not only Cwen – they're all gone. All of the children. All of the other nuns." The woman was crying but her eyes also betrayed fury. "It doesn't bear thinking about what they will go through. What their lives will be like now. Those children were meant to grow up to be thegns, and ladies of great houses, but now ... they'll be slaves grovelling at the feet of those monsters for scraps of food. Used and abused at whim by those Godless creatures. Traded for silver and worked until they die without a Christian word said over their graves."

"No," Merwynn wailed. "We have to save them, we have to fetch them back. There has to be something we can do?"

"You know there is not."

"Please," Merwynn begged, desperate to find some resolution. There had to be a way. "What about their parents, the villagers, the local thegns? We could gather the men and chase them down?"

Merwynn grabbed her cloak and made to leave but the woman stepped in front of her barring her exit. She slapped Merwynn hard across the face, "And how would we find them across the ocean? By now they have been taken to the long boats and have already set sail. No fyrd can fetch them back now, even if one could be raised. Not even God can help them now."

Merwynn stood in limbo as a desperate helplessness engulfed her. She collapsed on the floor weeping, the tears flowing freely into her hands. It was all her fault. She could have saved Cwen if she had only reached out to her. Even if she had been captured as well, she would at least have provided those children with some comfort as they were taken away. Merwynn hated herself for her cowardice and betrayal. She tore at the skin of her treacherous arms digging her nails in deep enough to draw blood. She wanted to tear the flesh from her bones.

The other nuns grabbed her arms and held her down. They tied her hands and feet to stop her thrashing around. In the end they forced her to drink a tincture which made her sleep.

When Merwynn awoke she no longer felt compelled to lash out but inside she had a self-loathing that threatened to consume her.

For days the five remaining nuns nursed their wounds and buried their dead. The young nun that Merwynn had seen violated in the kitchens had been unconscious but came around after two days. She had lost an eye and could not move her jaw but she had survived. Merwynn found it hard to look at her without feeling even more shame for leaving the girl to her fate too.

People from the nearby villages came to help them and provided blankets and food but it was clear that they could not remain at the ruined monastery.

Merwynn was a different person, quiet and withdrawn but it was the same with the other nuns. Together they decided to travel north to Whitby to join the double monastery of Streoneshalch - also founded by Hilda – one that housed monks and nuns together. This was a monastery that had higher walls and bigger numbers. Somewhere where they should be safe.

~ 7 ~

Stoned

Catherine was determined to show her manager that she was dedicated and hardworking even if she had been late back from her morning off. He was a good boss, the kind that never criticised or put her down. The worst thing he would ever do in the early days was to tell her that he was 'disappointed' and that was enough of a crushing blow from someone that she respected and who had given her an opportunity to develop her career.

She was so busy that afternoon playing catchup that she didn't think about the day's activities until the evening.

A couple of years earlier she had bought a nice two-bedroom flat, and the second bedroom allowed her to rent out a room, helping to pay the mortgage. She got home knowing that her flatmate, Liam would be out, but wanting to talk to him about the hypnosis session as well as having met Edward again. Liam was a good pal and someone that she depended on. They moved in different social circles, which in some ways made it the perfect relationship.

Liam was a tall lanky bearded geek with a passion for purple and collecting things. He was weird and wonderful and her closest friend with no physical attraction between them. Other women seemed to find him irresistible though, and he dated several at a time, all of whom knew about each other and were similar free spirits to himself. Liam didn't believe in restricting himself to a single monogamous relationship. He was at least honest about it and never misled any unsuspecting girl into something she was not happy with. Having said that, Liam had been spending a lot of time with a new girl more recently, Jojo.

Usually, Catherine liked Liam's friends but this girl was different. She was a psychiatric nurse and a complete know-it-all. Whenever she was in the flat Catherine found herself being told how the central heating was set too high, that she should let the wine breath for at least one hour before drinking it, and that she should go to bed earlier to avoid dry skin. Jojo even had advice on how to boil an egg. Throughout it all, Jojo was infuriatingly nice whenever she said these things so it left no room for any come-back that you could give her. Had she been Catherine's girlfriend she would have throttled her very early on. Liam, however, was far more patient and took it all within his lanky stride.

Catherine and Liam were opposite in the outlook on life, Catherine the more controlled and confined, Liam more fluid and open to creative expression in all its forms. Their friendship met firmly in the middle.

Catherine walked through the door, kicked off her shoes and went straight to the cupboard for a glass of red wine. It had been a long day. She was settled on the couch watching TV, her feet curled under her, and a glass cradled in one hand, when Liam came in – thankfully without Jojo in tow. He looked hassled and wet through from the rain that had started falling again shortly after she had got home.

She knew better than to try talking to him when he was distracted and so looked over her shoulder and announced, "The wine's breathing if you want a glass."

Liam wouldn't care if the wine had been breathing for a month, it was usually just opened and drunk, but it was a way of telling him that she wanted to talk.

After a few minutes he came into the living room with a towel around his neck and poured a large glass to the brim for himself. He pulled out his rolling tobacco, his Rizla papers, his lighter and his small cellophane wrapped block of hash. Each item was put ritually down on the tray in front of him.

With the TV running but, as usual, pretty much ignored, they talked about nothing in particular. Liam commented about the rain as he started to roll a joint with the expert precision of a man who did this at least 15 times a day.

Liam lit the joint and sat back in his chair looking relaxed.

"Rough day?" Catherine asked.

"Nope, not really," he said looking at the joint and taking another toke. Liam worked as a lighting designer and technician for the theatres in Edinburgh. He was freelance but had been working with one theatre lately and the politics of being stationed at one place for too long sometimes got to him. "What about you?" he asked.

"Weird," she replied. "I went for that hypnosis session about Tynemouth."

"Oh yeah," he said sitting forward with a more animated expression on his face. "How did that go?"

She told him about the session and how it had turned out so differently from what she had expected. As always Liam listened with interest and didn't even look surprised. He offered the joint to Catherine and, unusually for her on a weeknight, she took a puff. She held it in her lungs for a few moments and then exhaled. She felt more relaxed straight away.

"Who knows, maybe it's all real - maybe I have lived before … in Tynemouth." She took another drag and started to laugh.

The whole situation seemed very funny and rather ridiculous. What on earth was she thinking of? Reincarnation? She was not sure she even believed in such things. She'd been brought up in the Church of Scotland, dutifully going to Sunday school every week. However, when she'd reached about 12 years old, she told her grandmother that what the church taught didn't seem right. That it seemed to contradict itself all the time. Her grandmother's response was to tell Catherine that if she was unsure of the church that maybe she should read the bible for herself. After that her grandmother had removed all the other books in her room and told her that she could only have them back once she had read the bible from cover to cover.

Catherine had the distinct impression that it was supposed to be a punishment but instead she found the book enlightening. She found that she had more respect for what the philosophers of the time had come up with – a philosophy of love and forgiveness in a time of 'an eye for an eye' – but it in turn gave her even less regard for the church itself and how it had interpreted the teachings into a means of controlling the populace.

As a teenager she started to research the subject and why the Romans had at first embraced Christianity, then converted the whole empire to it. They chose selected gospels which taught the populace to behave the way it suited the people in power, and put them into one book, the bible. Then they built places of beauty and awe, churches for the ordinary people unlike anything they had ever been allowed to enter before. Beautiful architecture with gold and silver, bright stained glass and exquisite sculpture – no wonder the population was enthralled with 'the power of God'.

The dope was having a good effect and Liam was right along there with her. One of the best things about smoking dope with someone she knew well was the way in which they moved through a conversation together, each 'getting' the other completely.

"So what do you think about reincarnation then? It doesn't fit with your logical agnostic beliefs, does it?" Liam grinned.

"No, not really. Don't get me wrong, I think Jesus existed and admire him as a philosopher. I think he talked a lot of sense. But he never stated that he was the only son of God - in fact he stated that 'We are ALL the children of God'. He had a good sense of personal responsibility – something rather radical for the time -which was what he tried to teach. That people should love each other and act with kindness towards their fellow man. But I still think that he was just a man. I don't believe in God, or heaven or the like."

After she had read the bible Catherine's grandmother had forced her to go back to church every Sunday saying that she could not possibly have understood it and needed even more 'guidance'. Catherine had no respect for the overbearing zealous minister after that and would correct his quotations under her breathe.

"So, what do you believe happens after death then?" Liam asked.

"Nothing, or rather I believe in nature, that a body disintegrates and goes back into the earth. I don't believe in a 'soul' or a part of your identity moving to a higher plane. Memories are physical electrical impulses interpreted by the synapses within the brain. When the body dies surely those electrical signals would die as well, along with what gives people their personality. So maybe pure energy continues but not the person themselves."

"But what if the energy contains traces of the person - what if there is an imprint on it - like the instincts, flashes of feeling, the powerful stuff that stays with us always!?" Liam was frowning. "If energy cannot be created then each new life is recycling energy that's been around before."

"Um…" she said trying to grasp what he was saying.

"Maybe it's not like one person is recycled into one new person. Maybe all the energy from all the people dying is pooled together, then bits come back out to start new life. But those bits retain all the various instincts and powerful memories of the previous 'hosts' - for want of a better word."

"Could be," Catherine said.

Liam offered her the joint again, but she refused with a shake of her head. He continued, "Maybe people are like rain. If you think of 'life' like the rain drop. The evaporated energy or moisture is blown by the wind into a cloud. Then some of it coalesces into an individual drop of rain - and that creation of a drop of rainwater is when a person is born. As the droplet falls it gathers particles and experiences – life - until it reaches the ocean. At which point it ceases to be a drop of rain any more - and we die. But although the drop is gone, all that it gathered is now part of the sea, it becomes 'the ocean'. No longer indistinguishable. Then the sun rises and the moisture evaporates starting the whole process again. But not with exactly the same combination of atoms or energy."

After a moment's pause, Liam started to laugh. Catherine had stopped with her glass of wine half-way back to the table. She had been fascinated by his description and hadn't noticed she'd was frozen mid-motion until now. She took a sip and then she choked on the wine, going into a full-on coughing fit.

Liam roared with laughter which made her giggle as well, only serving to make the coughing worse.

~ 8 ~

Wild Dancing

A day later Catherine got a phone call from Edward asking her out that coming Tuesday.

"I go to a weekly Ceroc dance club and wondered if you'd like to join me."

Catherine laughed. Her? Dance?

"It's rather like a cross between jive and Latin-American. And at the club you get to learn it from beginners to advanced. Plus I would get to show you how to do some of the moves my sister Fiona and I were doing at the party."

Catherine remembered the pang of jealousy she had felt about being able to dance that way. "What a great idea! When and where?"

When the evening arrived, she had butterflies in her stomach. She was so nervous about doing something new that she didn't think about it being an actual 'date'. She tried on a dress but thought better of it, going back to her old faithful black jeans and sleeveless top.

She met Edward at the entrance to the club.

"Hi," he said as he reached out, touching her arm.

"Hi, right back at you," she quipped.

"Shall we go in? You're going to love this!"

His unrestrained enthusiasm was endearing even if he did remind Catherine of an over excited puppy.

Edward guided Catherine through the doors and the music hit her first. It was loud and energetic with a heavy swing beat. A great swathe of people were all dancing in couples on the floor. Women were spinning and being thrown in the air, turning in and out of their dance partners arms. The air was heavy and almost damp with their exertions, but it was intoxicating rather than off-putting. Everywhere around her, people loved what they were doing - they were passionate about their dancing and there were very few people standing around the edges of the room. Those that were hovering at the sides were gulping down from litre bottles of water and rubbing the moisture off their faces with towels from their bags. Not one person was sitting down. Clearly, they were ALL here to dance.

Catherine had never seen anything like this before. She had been to her fair share of nightclubs but this kind of partner dance was fascinating to watch and she was already hooked. She ached to be able to dance like they did.

Edward tapped her on the shoulder and leaned in to shout above the music, "You like it?"

"Yes!" she yelled back.

"Let's dance!"

Before she could reply he had grabbed her coat and thrown it over a chair, pulling her onto the dance floor.

Edward was an exceptional dancer. Although Catherine had no idea where she was going or what she was doing, he showed her the basics in about two minutes flat. He held her hand lightly in his and when he raised it above her head she turned underneath it, when he threw her hand to the side she would spin around and he expertly caught her and turned her again in another direction. She was dizzy but Edward was so proficient that it didn't worry her at all. Then as the end of the third song came around, he spun her three times, threw her backwards over his knee and caught her in a left arm dip which left her breathless.

They were both laughing as he brought her upright again and the song had finished.

"Hey," he said. "You're not bad for a beginner! I knew you had it in you."

"Thanks," she said dryly as a new song started, and they weaved their way through the spinning dancers towards the bar.

"How long have you been doing Ceroc?"

"About four years," he said. "I started when my sister dragged me along. I was pretty nervous at first, but they hold classes in the early part of the evening and I got better at it each week. It's pretty easy to do - once you have an idea of the moves."

Catherine was beginning to find Edward rather attractive. He had a strange, mocking sense of humour but he seemed a pretty solid bloke who, for some inexplicable reason, seemed to like her. She found it intriguing and confusing at the same time. She couldn't shake the feeling that she was only biding her time until he bored of her, but in the meantime, she would enjoy the attention.

Edward ordered two pints of water for them, which Catherine found odd as she would much rather have had a pint of beer but accepted the drink after their exertions. Edward drank over half of his in one gulping draft.

Then as they turned away from the bar, a girl bounded up and grabbed Edward by the arm. "Come on, this is my favourite song," she said as she pulled him towards the dance floor.

Catherine found it surprising but it seemed to be the etiquette of the place because Edward looked over his shoulder and handed her his pint glass saying, "Do you mind?"

Although it sounded as if he was asking if she would hold his glass, she got the impression that he was asking if she minded him dancing with another girl. Strangely enough, she didn't mind as it gave her a chance to rest, and to watch. Plus, she found the question rather flattering.

Catherine watched as they practically ran onto the floor and started dancing around the room. The girl was experienced and the joy on her face as she whirled and almost flew through the air was evident. She was wearing a short skirt which flowed in a circle each and every time she turned. On occasion Edward would use this flowing fabric to emphasise a spin by patting it higher into the air. It made Catherine regret not wearing the dress that she had tried on earlier in the evening. Edward was a much better dancer than she had thought; he had clearly been going easy on her as a beginner.

Catherine was impressed and, she had to admit to herself, once again a little envious of them dancing together - not of his attention, but of their skill. She wanted to dance like that. She wanted that wild abandon, and physical expression of pure joy. She'd got the bug.

Edward left the girl on the dance floor after a couple of songs. Then he came back to Catherine.

"There are more girls who come to the club than guys so the blokes who can dance are in high demand," he told her between quick gulps of water. "The girls tend to ask the guys to dance rather than the other way around. It's considered quite rude for a guy to refuse."

Edward was kept very active throughout the evening. He spent some time dancing with Catherine but each time they went for a break another girl would drag him off. It became funny and she could see why Edward drank water as soon as he got it in his hand. Soon Catherine managed to work out that after the pint of water she would have time to grab a quick gin and tonic before he got back again!

The evening was fun and she learnt a huge amount within a short space of time. She could dance, at a basic level at least, by the end of the night. Although it was only 10.30pm when they left Edward had been dancing for three hours solid without much of a break. He looked flushed and exhilarated and Catherine had genuinely enjoyed the evening.

"We're all going for a drink at the local now. Would you like to come?" he asked as he stripped off his t-shirt and pulled a clean dry one out of his bag.

He was leaner than she had imagined. It was all she could do not to reach out and put her hands on him.

"Oh, yes. A drink. Why not," she said as she pretended to look the other way.

Edward laughed at her again.

They went with about twelve of the other dancers to a local pub for half an hour before closing time and she was introduced to some of his friends.

They were a good crowd of people, from a variety of walks of life but all brought together through a passion for dancing. She felt a little on the outside as they chatted away but was happy to sit back and listen. Edward seemed very popular as everyone talked to him. He told jokes and was the centre of attention for the whole group. However, Catherine noticed that one petite woman in the crowd was giving Edward big-eyed, sulky looks from under blond curly locks of hair. However, Edward hadn't seemed to even notice her. Catherine wondered if this was someone that had a torch for him but thought it best not to ask.

After about half an hour Catherine started to feel her muscles seizing up. So she leaned over and said to Edward, "It has been a while since I've exerted so much energy and I am exhausted. I think it's time for me to go."

Edward smiled warmly, "You get used to it." He touched her arm, "Come again next week?"

"I'd love to," she replied with genuine enthusiasm.

"A week is a long time though, would you like to go to The Stand Comedy Club with me this weekend as well?"

Catherine smiled, "Yes, I'd love to do that as well."

~ 9 ~
Brotherly Love

Streoneshalch Monastery at Whitby was a whole new world for Merwynn. It was a large compound with bigger buildings made from stone – some left over from when the Romans had once lived there, hundreds of years before. It was imposing, formal and constrained. There were communal halls for eating and a hospital for the sick, a bakery, a pottery, a smithy, and a tannery as well as vegetable and physic gardens, farm animals, beehives etc. The monastery was a bustling community all within one compound.

The nuns were housed in individual cells within larger buildings instead of two or three to a small house like they were in Hackness. For the first time in her life Merwynn had some privacy, which was supposed to allow her time to search her soul, commune with God and find humility. But instead she felt cut off and alone. Her cell had a small, shuttered window which was not big enough to escape from and a low wooden stool in the corner. Beside the stool was a small chest which contained spare items of clothing, and some personal belongings like her mother's cloak. The stone walls of her small cell were cold and hard, but the straw bed that took up almost half the room was comfortable and she tried to make the best of it.

Her life was ruled by bells at Whitby. Bells to wake you for prayers. Bells to tell you that food was ready. Bells to order you to work, or to indicate time to rest again. Each bell brought back that moment of panic in the Hackness monastery, and with it the huge wave of guilt she still felt. Gradually she got used to the noise, but the alarm never quite left her and she jumped each time the bells peeled.

Merwynn worked in the pottery but relished any opportunity to visit the smithy where the monks were making anything from scythes to fine silver and metal work. She was struck by the smell the first time she visited it. It was hot and dusty but smelt like earth and fire rolled together. The acrid smell of the coal mixed with the sweet smell of red-hot iron was intoxicating. The air was sharp with the tension of expanding and shrinking metals. She was fascinated with how these artists could make something that was unbreakable and solid flow like water into other shapes and then magically go back to being frozen and impenetrable again.

It was their silver work that she was most impressed by. They were skilled jewellers and the objects they produced were a sight to see – detailed and breathtaking in their beauty. Merwynn would ask to inspect their work with feigned indifference as she picked up and admired a stunning jewelled silver cross bound for a cathedral in the south. To hold such riches in her hands was incredible. She was envious of the monks who got to work with such materials, whereas her hands were only allowed to work with clay. But the smithy was hot and the work was hard, so maybe she didn't have such a raw deal.

"What do you think of this one?" a monk by the name of Adalbert handed her a simple silver ring.

Merwynn gasped as she turned the ring over in her young hand. The two overlapping ends of the ring were coiled into small spirals, just like her stone snake. It was simple, but beautiful at the same time.

Adalbert leaned in close and whispered, "I made it for you."

Merwynn was taken aback, "For me?"

She had no idea what to do or say as she looked at the man. She had hardly even noticed him before. He was only a little taller than her and a few years older. He had the wide strong shoulders of a smith, his brown hair was thick and his face red from the heat of the forge. There was a tantalising danger about him though, a spark that she had never experienced before, and could not explain.

Adalbert smiled as she flushed red, and he closed her hand over the ring. A bell tolled for prayers and Merwynn jumped. Adalbert took a protective step towards her.

"Quick," he said, "hide it before any of the others see it. Keep it safe, and when you wear it, think of me."

Merwynn walked away from the smithy in shock. When she got back to her cell, she was surprised to see that she still had the ring in her closed fist. She spent the time she should have been in silent prayer turning it over in her hand and trying it on different fingers. She knew she couldn't wear it but possessing it was delightful. She put it in the pocket alongside the stone snake.

After that, every time she saw Brother Adalbert her heart would beat faster. She would glance up and see his hawkish brown eyes gazing into her soul, and it aroused feelings in her she had not been aware of before. Those eyes seemed to hunt her and she felt drawn to him. Each time she caught him watching her she got a jolt like the slap of cold water. She had to fight the urge to reach out to him, to touch his face.

As they passed in the cloister almost within touching distance her legs quivered making her stumble. She only just managed to stop herself from falling over. The nun beside her caught Merwynn's arm, her face showing concern and a silent rebuke for clumsiness, but she didn't say a word.

All About Love

Two days later Catherine was back in Dr Rayal's office for her second session. As she arrived, she realised she was much more comfortable with him than she had on the first occasion. Bastian smiled as he collected her from the reception area and asked how her week had gone.

"Pretty well. I went dancing a couple of nights ago and really rather enjoyed myself."

"Excellent," he said with an upbeat tone to his voice, but also with a finality that Catherine perceived was to prevent her launching into conversation about it. She was paying for his time after all and it was clear that he wanted to keep it all very professional. Catherine was happy with that.

He gestured to the recliner and she sat down.

"So what did you think about your last session?" He asked.

"I'm not sure. It is almost like the subject is too big to be contained inside my small head." She laughed at her inadequacy to articulate her feelings.

Bastian smiled but didn't laugh with her. "I'm not sure that I follow you, can you explain what you mean?"

She felt very unsure of herself, like she had been rebuked by a teacher, so was quick to answer. "I remember the hypnosis session like it happened. It seems like a memory now rather than a dream. In fact over the last week I have woken up several times having dreamt about it, but I can't seem to grasp what it was all about."

"Ah," Bastian said leaning forward with his elbows on his knees and his fingers lightly touching in front of his chin. "I've heard that before. Hypnosis is not the same as dreaming. Dreams are jumbles of ideas and images which the brain interprets whilst in an unconscious state - which you then try to interpret and put into perspective on awaking. Hypnosis on the other hand is experienced in a relaxed state - but still within consciousness enough to be reflected upon at the time. Hypnosis is accessing memory, but memory enhanced by being viewed in a super-conscious state."

She felt distinctly uneasy and not sure she understood him at all – how could a super-conscious state show her memories of someone else's life. She paused for a moment before asking. "So how does this all relate to a random memory of visiting Tynemouth as a teenager? Why did that take me back to another life? And what was I running away from?"

"There is something there that connects everything. Your mind is trying to tell you something. But it needs to put the foundations in so that the message has a firm footing. It might be that your subconscious is showing you that no matter what disguise you wear, you cannot escape your past."

"I don't understand."

Bastian smiled, radiating calm. He sat back opening his palms to the ceiling, "Neither do I ... yet. That's why we have to delve deeper. When we understand where this leads you, then we will understand the connection."

She paused to take on board what he was saying, but before she could ask any further questions about it, he moved the subject on.

"Well, let's see where this takes us today, shall we?"

She swallowed the queries that had arisen, not wanting to appear stupid, and leaned back on the recliner.

"I think we should go back a bit further to see if we can find out why you were at the Priory in the first place?"

"Ok."

Once again, he put on the music and started to talk. "Close your eyes and relax. You are safe here. Sink into the chair. Feel the tension seep out of you as you each part of your body relaxes further. Feel the warmth in your toes relaxing as all the tension evaporates from them. You can feel a warmth as the muscles release and each part of your body relaxes further ..."

Catherine found that she fell into a relaxed state much more easily. She was drifting in a floaty feeling of lightness within only a few seconds of listening to his mellow voice. The everyday stresses and thoughts seeped away and she was left suspended in a misty stairwell. She started to descend the stairs again, faintly seeing the doorway below her.

As she reached for the door handle, she saw her own hand involuntarily hesitate before gripping it and turning.

She sat alone on a smooth wooden stool. Her head was lowered and she stared at her hands that were clasped in her lap. She concentrated hard to contain a rage that she would never be allowed to express.

"Where are you?" Came the voice.

"I am in my father's hall."

"Are you still dressed as a man?"

Perplexed by the question she looked down at herself and saw a dress which was her mothers before her. It was a rich dark red colour and was held in place by two brooches, one on each shoulder, linked together with beaded necklace. She wore a belt which was knotted and from which small tools and a pouch hung. Underneath the woollen dress she could feel the linen shift which protruded from the sleeves, laced from elbow to wrist. On her head she could feel the loosely tied wrap that covered her long dark hair.

"No, I am dressed as always."

"Can you describe your surroundings?"

She looked around. She was sitting in the middle of a large room. Beside her was another more ornate stool carved with patterns and swirls which gave it a special place in the hall. The wooden floor was cold beneath her thin leather shoes and she was automatically sitting with her heels raised to avoid the chilly contact. Daylight was coming in through three small panes of what looked like slivers of yellowish polished horn which had been slotted into horizontal posts of wood. As a result the light was muted but adequate to see by.

In the middle of the hall was a square firepit surrounded by an even set of stones, and although it was lit, was burning very low awaiting being built up for the evening.

At either end of the hall she could see wicker partitions behind which there were wooden sleeping pallets and tables. The walls themselves seemed to be made of wooden beams and some kind of plaster between, though it was difficult to tell in the dim light. More than three quarters of the wall area was covered in fabrics – what looked like rough tapestries and wall hangings. The ceiling showed the thatch in need of some repair and she was irked at it remaining the way it was.

The door at one end of the hall was open to the bright spring daylight outside, which made the hall seem all the more dark and smoky. She would not usually be inside at this time and she felt defiant with inactivity.

"It's cold. There's some wooden furniture. There are hangings on the walls and a low fire in the room."

"Are you alone?"

"Yes, blessedly," she sighed.

"What troubles you?" said the voice.

"My father has chosen me a husband whom I do not wish to marry."

She had a mix of feelings bubbling up from the pit of her stomach. Grief, excitement, resentment, and a feeling of suppressed rage. How dare he treat her like this.

"Can you refuse?"

She wanted to cry, to reach out and find the arms of her mother. Her throat tightened and tears pricked her eyes. Her mother. 'Modor,' she corrected. Images flashed into her memory of warm cuddles, of tickling and giggling, laughing and singing together, of love and a feeling that she mattered. She mattered very much.

A movement caught her eye and she looked up to see the open door to the bright sunshine outside. There in the doorway stood a silhouetted cat, staring at her, its head titled to one side. Then with a flick of its dark tail, turned and walked out of sight.

"Yes," she said. "Yes, I can."

"What are you doing now?"

She got up and smoothed down the front of her dress.

"I am getting up," She pulled a thick black woollen cloak up over her shoulders with a deep comforting hood. The cloak was warm and made by her mother who had oiled the wool against the weather with her own hand. It was the only thing she would take from her father's hall.

"I am leaving."

Back in Bastian's office Catherine found tears rolling down her cheeks. Bastian handed her a tissue and she wiped them away. Confused by the onset of emotion.

Nothing major seemed to have happened but Bastian was most intrigued by what she hadn't mentioned whilst under hypnosis: the details that she had noticed and the mother she had remembered so vividly.

It was as if it had just happened: the feeling of powerlessness and hopelessness remained with her. The feelings for her father who seemed to care so little for her happiness – she was not hurt by his behaviour as if it was somehow expected. She strangely knew that he didn't see women in that way, that they were commodities rather than other human beings. He wasn't a 'bad man' per se just an ignorant man quite natural for his time.

Bastian brought her back to the topic at hand. "Did you get an impression of what was outside? Where you were geographically?"

"No, I couldn't see. It was too bright to see anything past the door."

"It sounds like quite a rich house though?" Bastian was leaning forward in his chair, fascinated.

"Yes, but it seemed to be old and shrinking somehow. The wall hangings looked faded, the fire was low, there were no rugs or carpets - just rush mats over floorboards. There seemed to be little there. I was a lot younger than the last session too." She could not articulate it but felt as if the family had fallen on hard luck. That somehow the girl had seen better times when things were more comfortable. The memory of her mother was situated within greater comfort and there had been better matting underfoot then. "There is one thing though, the cloak! It was the same cloak as I was wearing in the first session, when I was older, and dressed as man. It was my mother's cloak and seemed very precious." The thought of the love the girl's mother had for her brought fresh tears to Catherine's eyes but she couldn't identify why.

"What was your relationship like with your own mother?" Bastian asked handing her another tissue.

"I didn't have one," Catherine replied more bitterly than she meant to. "My mother was never a mum to me. I was just something to be dumped on my grandmother whilst she went out partying. Far more interested in going out and enjoying herself."

Bastian didn't say a word but made a barely audible 'hmm' sound.

Catherine didn't look up. She changed the subject, "What do you think this all means – the room, the clothes, the cat? And why am I seeing these things?" She paused, surprised that she was going to ask the next question, "Is she, *me*, in a previous life?"

To her surprise Bastian didn't laugh at her, instead he frowned and then started to talk.

"It's very rare, but there are certain characters who are so strong, or events that happen in a life that is so cataclysmic, that they cannot rest. These … souls, for want of a better word … continue to look for answers. For a lost beloved, for forgiveness, or for vengeance - hundreds, even thousands of years after their death. It's possible that you've resonated with a spirit from another former life who is looking for resolution in a similar way." He moved forward in his seat. "There will be some connection with your life now, something that connects you from this life experience. I wouldn't say that you are *reincarnated* from them, but that a part of them has connected with a part of you and that thread needs to be explored to its end - before either of you will have any peace."

"So we have to keep digging?" Catherine sighed.

"I think it will all become clear if we keep looking deeper."

Their time was up and Catherine had to get back to work. However, before she left, she booked a block of sessions with Bastian. Something in her subconscious was trying to tell her something and she was determined to listen.

~ II ~

Arousal

Merwynn found herself thinking about Brother Adalbert all the time. As the days turned, she found excuses to visit the smithy – tools that the pottery needed repairing, a broken key, a kitchen knife that needed a new handle. Brother Adalbert was always there, smiling whenever he saw her. She would blush and then smile back. They were only a few snatched minutes in the day but they were precious to her.

Over time he would encourage her to look closer at pieces he was working on. A gold necklace for an ealdorman's daughter, or a broach for a local thegn. The skill he had with precious metal was enticing and people came far and wide to pay for his art. There were silver crosses as well, created for monasteries all over Northumbria and elsewhere. Merwynn was impressed and would reach out to touch the shining silver with wonder.

Adalbert would put his hand on top of hers and stroke it with his thumb. "You are so beautiful," he would whisper. "Your visits are such a treasure. Nothing here can compare."

Merwynn was adrift, she knew that touching was forbidden, but it felt so right. Stolen moments which sent shock waves through Merwynn. It was like an animal inside her had awoken and was demanding to be fed. She hungered for his attention, and for his touch.

On one such visit the other smiths were absent having gone to deal with a farm plough that needed a blade replacing. Adalbert took Merwynn aside and held her up against the wall of the smithy. He kissed her firmly on the mouth, pushing his tongue in and groping her breasts over her dress. Merwynn was shocked but also excited. Then, as she started to respond, he stopped and pulled away again.

"You have me under a spell," he moaned. "I cannot live without you. You are cruel to tempt me and leave me so encumbered."

Merwynn didn't even know what he meant. She left confused and avoided the smithy for days. Then she was told by the nuns to deliver some tools that needed mending. She had no idea what reception she would have from Adalbert and was nervous that he would reject her.

Adalbert looked forlorn when she arrived. His eyes followed her as she crossed the ground and she could feel the longing in his gaze. He sent the other smith away to deliver some tools and used the snatched moments to talk to her.

"I have missed you," he whispered close to her ear, his breath hot on her neck. "I must have you. Tomorrow. I cannot wait any longer. Come and give me a sign that we can be together."

Merwynn said nothing but simply delivered the tools and left. All night she thought about what he had said. What sign did he want from her? She had come to crave his attention, wanted his touch. Already she knew that he could have anything he wanted from her.

The next day Merwynn found herself with her back against the outside wall behind the smithy scraping up and down; brother Adalbert's two hands grasping her bare buttocks and pulling her off the ground. All this was done in silence, not a word was spoken as he grunted and moaned his pleasure. She had courted this, had wanted it as much as him, and she was revelled in the animal passion which engulfed them both.

~ 12 ~

Comedy

The following evening was Catherine's date with Edward. She had wondered several times whether he would change his mind about the date - maybe he was being kind by offering to take her to the comedy club and would find a reason to cancel.

However, on the Friday morning she got a text which said, "Looking forward to seeing you tonight – meet be at the entrance to The Stand on Queen Street at 9pm?"

"Ok," she wrote back. "I have heard great things about The Stand so I am hoping it lives up to its reputation!"

They met in front of the Comedy Club just off Queen Street and he was waiting for her when she arrived at 9.01pm.

"You're late!" he remarked with a smile as he kissed her on the cheek. Shall we?"

They went down the stairs into the basement bar. Edward had already bought the tickets, so they went straight past the queue at the door and inched towards the bar through a room crammed to bursting point with people. He bought drinks and they found a niche standing around the right side of the stage.

They had to huddle together in the crowd and as soon as the acts started up all conversation ceased.

The stand-up comics were either utterly brilliant or totally awful. The ones who didn't capture the audience within the first minute were heckled and even booed off stage. It was brutal. The audience were merciless, and Catherine felt for those poor comedians who were doing their best to entertain this carnivorous unyielding mob. The good comedians however were hysterical and could pick on members of the audience with equal cruelty. It gave Catherine some satisfaction to see that the good comedians targeted the very people who were cruel to the less experienced ones. There seemed to be some justice in it, but never before had she so respected the people who got up on stage and tried to perform as a stand-up comic. She knew she couldn't do it – they must have balls of brass!

Edward and Catherine laughed at the same jokes and seemed to be in sync with each other. Catherine found herself laughing in unison with Edward at the same jokes. It felt like they were in perfect harmony, their senses of humour perfectly aligned. The crowded space seemed to press them closer together, their bodies touching subtly and frequently in a natural way, given the lack of space.

After the comedians' show ended, they had time to have a quick drink before the club closed. Edward managed to find a vacant table and they sat closely together talking about the evening - replaying some of the more acidic comments. Whilst they sat there Edward's knee was pressed against hers and she wasn't altogether sure if it was intentional. She liked it though. Tentatively she allowed herself to think that maybe, just maybe, he liked her too. Though she couldn't think for the life of her why.

When the club closed and they were ushered out, Edward waited with Catherine on Queen Street whilst she hailed a cab. The air was chilly and it seemed that the summer was over.

She shivered and remarked: "Och weel, it's a braw nicht the nicht!" to which Edward laughed and held her hands rubbing warmth into them.

As the cab drew up Edward pulled her closer to him and wrapped his arms around her as if they were dancing. Then he planted his lips on her and gave her a huge smacking comic kiss.

As he let go of her, Catherine pretended a pout, "Is that all I get?"

To which he smiled with satisfaction and again wrapped his arms around her. This time he kissed her passionately and she felt her lower abdomen tighten. His lips were soft and the kiss passionate whilst at the same time being gentle. She wanted it to go on forever, but the taxi driver had other ideas and hooted the horn – breaking the mood entirely.

They broke apart laughing and Catherine fumbled for the taxi door handle.

"Ceroc on Tuesday?" Edward said through the open door.

"Of course," she smiled, and the taxi drove off as soon as the door closed.

Liam was still up when she got home. He was ensconced in his room working out dungeons and dragons strategies for his gaming the next day. He took his Dungeon Master responsibilities very seriously but stopped to talk to Catherine and find out how her date went. He opened a bottle of wine and poured her a glass.

"So? Give!" he said.

"Well ..." she kicked off her shoes and curled up on the couch as she started to tell him about her evening. She told him all about the comedy club and the banter, how they had been in close contact in the club and some of the more interesting comedians. She also told him about the kiss and how it made her feel.

"Sounds like a pretty good date. How come you didn't bring him home with you?"

She threw a cushion at him, which he caught with a laugh.

"Well," he said, "you could've at least have offered! It has been a long time since you got any."

Admonishing Liam on his loose morals Catherine finished her wine and asked him about his day. Then she wound her way to bed. She was elated but exhausted as she threw her clothes off and brushed her teeth. Before she snuggled down to sleep, she checked her phone and saw a text from Edward. She squinted in the darkness at the brightly lit screen and read it.

Goodnight Catherine – I had a wonderful time tonight! x

Catherine fell asleep still smiling.

The images flashed in and out of focus. She walked along a vaulted corridor which was open to the courtyard on one side, with a stone wall on the other. Embedded in the wall, every few feet, were arched windows, glazed in coloured glass with lead outlines. It was stained glass, something that she was still in awe of. She tried to see the images out of the corner of her eye as she kept her head dutifully bowed in obedience.

She was not alone. Around her there were several others, all of them dressed as she was. A plain blue tunic dress belted with a cord at the waist from which hung a leather pouch; a linen headdress covering her head and neck; and over this she was wearing another veil and her cloak over her shoulders against the chill winter wind which blew across the courtyard.

Catherine found that she was dreaming this dream more and more. It was always the same - walking along a corridor - but the light would be different, sometimes she wore the cloak sometimes she didn't. One time she was simply standing in the corridor staring at the stained glass and marvelling at its beauty.

Awaking to the alarm the next morning Catherine lay perplexed at the images, trying to remember her surroundings and what the dream might mean. Then it faded and the day-to-day thoughts crept back in. Edward popped into her head and she smiled.

She liked what was happening with Edward. He was such a laid-back person and was open and friendly with everyone he met. He seemed to be the kind of charismatic bloke that everyone liked and she was flattered that it was her he seemed interested in. Catherine had never considered herself a beauty. She kept herself fit and healthy, she was well proportioned, and all her features were in the right place – but the whole was nothing special. She took care to dress well, ensuring her make up was immaculate and every hair was in place. Making 'the best' of herself as her grandmother had taught her – outward appearances being so very important. She was good at her job, and courteous to everyone she met, and was even quite good at hiding her shyness. At the same time, she knew deep down that she was nothing special. Nothing that made her interesting to someone like Edward.

Edward on the other hand behaved with her like she was the most attractive person on earth and that every moment he spent with her was wonderful. It was quite intoxicating and an attractive personality trait in him. She had noticed at Ceroc, that he had this effect on most people around him as well.

Catherine felt on top of the world, and for all her 'take your time before jumping in' sensibilities, still found herself thinking about Edward more and more. She had to admit that she could be falling for him.

HINDSIGHT

"Back to the real world," she glanced at the clock. Running late again. She dragged herself out of bed and got into the usual morning routine – as always, coffee first before jumping in the shower and a mad dash to get ready for work. On her second sip of coffee she stopped dead and groaned aloud. She remembered that it was Saturday and, berating herself for not turning off the alarm, went back to bed.

~ 13 ~

It's In His Kiss

Catherine's relationship with Edward developed quickly. They started dancing twice a week and then saw each other on weekends as well. The dancing was invigoration and exciting. She had good rhythm and, as long as she was dancing with a bloke who knew what he was doing, could hold her own. However, she still spent most of the evening downing gin and tonics whilst she watched Edward dance with other more energetic women.

Edward said that everyone who went at Ceroc was 'damaged' in some way, and although she'd been surprised by the comment at first, she knew what he meant. Most people were divorced or had some drastic story to tell. They were a myriad group of interesting souls who had all lived, loved and lost along the way. They danced for fun, to express their joy for life and to share a non-committed intimate contact with another soul for as long as the music lasted. The expression used was that Ceroc was 'the vertical expression of the horizontal intention' and it was the most flirtatious of dances.

There were of course those people who only went dancing to pick up a partner. There were a few men on the prowl who treated it as a hunting ground, but those people were identified by the regular dancers and as long as they danced, they were accepted by the rest. No-one interfered nor did they warn unsuspecting victims that a charmer's attentions were commonplace. Like an unwritten code of conduct that you minded your own business about what happened after the dance was over.

When Catherine arrived the next week, Edward was already on the dance floor swinging a new girl around as he showed her the moves. He was watching out for her though and waved with enthusiasm from across the dance floor only moments after Catherine walked in.

At the end of the song he bowed politely to the girl and led her to the side of the dance floor then came bounding over to Catherine.

"Hi," he said kissing her full on the mouth. "Come dance." He grabbed her hand and pulled her down the two steps onto the dance floor.

She had to take her coat off and throw it to the side as she moved. The 'Shoop Shoop' song by Cher was playing and they whirled around to the sexy beat of the music. The lyrics made her grin like a child as they seemed so appropriate. The worries and stresses of the work day melted away, and she felt so much better. She was caught up in the beat, the swinging bodies around her, and Edward. He was laughing as they danced and seemed so happy to see her. His enthusiasm was infectious and her tiredness evaporated. She was having fun.

They danced for six songs in a row until she couldn't dance any more. Smiling, and out of breath, she pushed Edward away and told him to find someone else to dance with. He was grabbed by another girl, and Catherine sidled off to the bar.

The bartender gave her the knowing smile and handed over the usual innocuous looking glass of fizzy 'water' and she took a grateful draft of the welcome beverage. Then she leaned over with an apologetic smile and asked for a pint of water as well. She was parched and knew that knocking down G&T's when thirsty was a bad idea. With a pout, the bartender handed her what she asked for.

"Just this once I promise!"

She watched Edward for a bit, still whirling and spinning on the dance floor. He was lifting a very good dancer into the air so that her legs pointed right up to the ceiling, then letting her fall and both of her legs went on one side of his hips, and then the other. They reminded her so much of 1950's dancers who she had seen on films and television – the jive and the jitterbug. It was fast and sexy and they seemed totally in sync with each other. She had a momentary pang of jealousy, but snapped out of it muttering, "Don't be so stupid Catherine. They're just dancing."

She looked around the room instead and started to people-watch a little. There were very few men not dancing. The women around the edges of the dance floor were flushed with their exertions and taking a break. Almost all of them were watching the dance floor or talking in pairs.

However, across the room Catherine caught sight of one woman who was pale in comparison to the others. She had not been dancing and seemed to be obsessively watching one couple. Catherine had seen the same girl the week before dancing with a flamboyant Frenchman. She looked through the crowd of dancers and saw him dancing with a jazzy looking leggy blond in a cut-off top. Even Catherine could see the expression of lust on his face and she looked back to the pale faced woman. The look of dejection said it all. There was more to that association than dancing and the girl was torturing herself by watching him develop a new relationship.

Catherine understood her but also thought she was rather pathetic. After all, she didn't have to come to the club and watch it all unfold in front of her. Mind you, would Catherine give up her new hobby because of a man?

Edward appeared in front of her again – his boundless energy still glowing like a beacon. "I need a shower!" Edward said wiping his face on the towel he had brought with him and changing into a clean t-shirt. "Want to join me?" he added with a wink, wrapping an arm around her waist.

"Another time," she said with a shy smile.

Edward had an early flight to London the next day so couldn't stay for a drink. He was going to be away for three days and would be back at the weekend.

"Will you go to Ceroc on Thursday?" he asked before he left.

"No, I don't think so. I don't want to stand there like a lemon. I saw a girl on her own tonight watching the French guy dancing with a blond – and she looked sad, and rather pitiful."

"You mean the guy with the long hair?"

"Yes, that's him."

"Yeah, I know him," he said with a frown. "That guy has done that to numerous girls. He uses the dancing to get women into bed then as soon as he has conquered them, he loses interest. It is like the dance is foreplay to him."

"What a shit."

"It is pretty low, but that's what some guys do. I've never seen the attraction of one-night stands. I've found the longer you stay with someone the better the sex gets."

Catherine felt an irresistible urge to hug him. "Really? You mean you're not a virgin?"

He growled, then laughed and pulled her into a hug. "Let's not go there huh? There is only you and me. What is past is past, okay? I was thinking, the weather is supposed to be nice this weekend, how about a walk along the beach?"

"Ok," she said as he leaned forward and kissed her passionately before disappearing out of the door. "See you at the weekend!" he waved as he trotted away.

93

With every hypnosis session, the details became increasingly vivid, drawing her deeper into a narrative that felt increasingly real. Each session wove a new tapestry of memories, so intricate and lifelike that they seamlessly blended with her own recollections, creating an ever-expanding mosaic of experiences. It was almost like an addiction as she started to look forward to the sessions more and more. Each time she went under hypnosis she was transported back to a world which was as real as the waking one. Her senses of sight, sound, touch, taste and even smell worked perfectly when she was under. She could smell the clear quality of the fresh air along with damp moss, wet tree trunks, and flowers from the surrounding forest mixed with the delicious cooking smells coming from the kitchens. Everything was solid and experienced as if it was happening right at that moment. When she came back to the present day and into Bastian's office, she remembered it so vividly with all the emotion that she had experienced whilst under hypnosis: none more so that after their third session.

She was walking head bowed along the familiar cloister which led from the nunnery to the church. From the other direction the monks came in single file and passed almost within touching distance. As she had often done before, she lifted her eyes as the monks passed to see a man looking at her with desire in his brown eyes. Their eyes locked and she had a strong desire to reach out to touch his face – but a part of her, deep inside, was also revolted, making her feel physically sick. She felt a remote self-loathing and fury at not being able to control her emotions. Her legs quivered and she stumbled in step, righting herself in time not to fall. Embarrassment was added to the self-loathing and it was almost too much to bear.

The now familiar voice told her to move on, to find another happier time.

The image was replaced by a scene of gruesome detail. Holding her hand out to a man, showing him a silver ring on her finger. Then leading him out and behind the smithy. His hands on her face, kissing and caressing. His hands on her breasts and between her legs. Her hands fumbling with the cassock and pulling up her skirts. Then her back against the wall scraping up and down. It was over in a flash, passionate, hot and heavy. On the outside she was satiated but, on the inside, she felt utter misery at herself. Not at her wanton behaviour, but horror at having let herself down and having started something she could not stop.

Catherine awoke from the session feeling used, dirty, and embarrassed - with a shame she had never experienced before. She came around crying, knowing that she had done a great wrong to herself. She had given into temptation and it would be the undoing of her.

Bastian talked to her and grounded her again – reminding her that this was all in the past. He brought Catherine out of her grief and back into the real world.

"There is nothing to be embarrassed about," he said. "This is something that needs to be remembered. This is part of what is haunting you and you need to go through this to get to the root of the story."

"I'm not embarrassed," she said, though she was a little. "I just feel a deep shame, like I have done something wrong. Like I am wrong."

"Firstly, what you are experiencing is not who you are now – remember it is a thread that connects you to someone in the past. Secondly, maybe this is something to do with the lesson you need to learn?"

Catherine felt strangely surreal. But somehow, she knew that they were getting somewhere, and perhaps if she stuck with it, she might understand why she had sensed a darkness coming after her.

As she left Dr Rayal's office she saw a familiar figure getting in the lift. "Fiona?" Catherine said quickening her step to catch the doors. She hadn't seen Edward's sister since that first meeting at the party.

"Oh," Fiona said looking a little alarmed. "Hello."

"What are you doing here?"

"I forgot my scarf this morning so popped back in to pick it up," she waved a bright coloured silk square at Catherine as the lift doors closed. "Have you been to see Bastian, er, Dr Rayal?" she asked.

"Yes, it's all a bit overwhelming but very interesting at the same time. I do feel like we are getting somewhere though."

"I know what you mean," Fiona smiled weakly. "He is a genius and has helped me so much. It all makes so much more sense now, and I can see why I had so much fear before. Stick with him, he knows what he's doing."

She seemed rather removed and a bit distant – talking in a normal tone of voice but not making eye contact.

Catherine got the distinct impression that something was not right. "Is everything okay?"

"Yes, yes, everything's fine," Fiona sighed, tucking the scarf into her bag, and looking at her watch. "Things on my mind is all." She smiled more warmly as the lift doors opened again and she started to walk away. "Must dash! But maybe we should get together with Edward sometime for a coffee?" she said over her shoulder.

"That would be … nice." Catherine's voice trailed off as Fiona disappeared out the door.

~ 14 ~
Dream Come True

The weather was indeed nice that weekend with the Autumn sun and a warm breeze making it a pleasant day to walk. Edward picked Catherine up at her flat and they drove to the coast in Gullane to a beautiful, secluded beach in East Lothian that he knew.

Edward reached out and took Catherine's hand as they walked along the sandy paths towards the beach, "So how are the hypnosis sessions going?"

"Interestingly." Catherine said with a finality that was not missed.

Edward grinned, "You're not going to tell me about them then?"

"Nope, I think I will keep that to myself," she smiled trying to imitate his impish grin. "Talking of which, how's your sister by the way?"

His face fell a little. "She's alright, though she's split up with her boyfriend Rick. They used to be so happy. She won't talk to me about it, but I know that there's something wrong."

"How awful. What do you think it might be? Do you think he did something? Perhaps he was unfaithful or something?"

"I'm not sure. If I thought that he'd hurt her at all I would have already paid him a visit. Truth is, I don't know what's wrong and there is little I can do if she won't talk to me."

"You're close the two of you – aren't you?"

"What, me and wee Fiona? Aye, we are. Though we used to fight like cat and dog when we were young. Fiona was the typical irritating little sister who followed me around and got under my feet." He paused and his face became more serious. "Then Dad died of cancer. It'd only been diagnosed a couple of weeks before, giving us no time to adjust to the idea. Mum never recovered from it. You rarely met a couple more devoted to each other. She followed him a couple of years later. She seemed to wither away. I was 18 years old at the time, and Fiona was only 15."

"How awful."

"My mum's official cause-of-death was 'heart attack' but she stopped living when Dad died. They were good parents. It was such a waste." He paused taking a deep breath and Catherine didn't know what to say.

After a moment of awkward silence Edward recovered himself and started again. "After that I felt responsible for Fiona and as a result our relationship changed – we became much closer. I was her guardian and it changed me too, made me more responsible than my friends were. We became each other's rock and I still try to look out for her. That's why this latest silence of hers troubles me."

"I met her a couple of days ago, coming out of the hypnotist's office. She was late for something, I think. She had to dash off."

"Yes, that would be my sister!" Edward laughed.

"She suggested that we meet up for a coffee. Maybe that would be a chance to see if she wants another woman to talk to. I'd love to get to know her."

Edward smiled, "Yes, we'll have to arrange that. It might help."

At that moment the grassy verges melted away at the end of the sandy path and the expanse of the beach was laid out before them. The golden sands glinting in the sun with the clear blue waters of the sea massaging the shoreline.

"Oh my," Catherine sighed, "this is beautiful."

They walked down to the waters edge and stood for a moment in silence before taking off their shoes and socks to paddle. The cold slap of the water was invigorating but not unpleasant on their warm skin - and carrying their shoes they walked ankle deep in the water along the beach.

"I do envy your relationship with your sister, I ... didn't have a family like other people do."

"You rarely talk about your family – we've been seeing each for over a month now and I think you've only ever mentioned them once. Do you not see them much?" Edward asked.

"No, not at all really. Not since leaving school."

Edward raised an eyebrow.

"Nothing untoward. I just felt that my grandmother, Eve, had done enough, so when I started uni ... it was a chance for her to get her life back. She hadn't ever wanted kids - her generation didn't get much choice about that though. My mum was an only child and Eve would have been free after she left home - if it wasn't for being left with me."

"Sounds pretty cold."

"She spent 30 years doing something she'd never wanted. She'd tried to raise my mother right, but it just got spat back in her face. My mother got pregnant with me whilst she was still at school - then she left Eve to pick up the pieces. Even telling people I was her sister rather than her daughter. When I was five my mum started nursing college and went out to work so I hardly saw her. It was Eve who took me to school for the first time – I remember vividly seeing all the mums and dads hugging their children goodbye and when I tried to do the same Eve just tutted at me and told me not to mess my clothes up. After her experience with my mother I think she just wanted to make sure she got it right this time." Catherine looked out to sea. "It could have been so much worse, Eve could have let me go into care, but she didn't. She raised me the best she knew how." Catherine was rather relieved that they were walking hand-in-hand looking out over the ocean – she didn't think that she would be able to articulate any of this if she had been talking to him face to face. It gave her the confidence to admit something she had never said out loud before, "As for my mum, well she never cared for me at all."

"Maybe she wasn't capable," Edward squeezed her hand, "there are some people who just don't know how."

"Oh, she knew how. She ditched me for good when I was 12. Got married to the first doctor she could get her hooks into and went on to have two boys, who - Eve tells me - she dotes on. It was just *me* that she didn't like." Catherine shrugged.

"What about your father?"

Catherine spoke in a very matter-of-fact tone, "Eve told me everything before I left for Uni – how Mum had been so difficult and such a handful. She said that mum had *'liked the boys'* too much. I doubt she even knew who my sperm-donor was. I did confront my mum once and insisted I had a right to know who my father was - when I was about 11. She slapped me. She told me that it made her sick to look at me and that I should never ask that again." Catherine paused, "She'd never been violent with me before. In fact, she hardly ever touched me at all."

Catherine was surprised the words were coming out of her mouth. The memory was painful and she resisted the urge to pull away from Edward - before he could reject her - and instead told her inner-self to trust him with it. Having started she knew she had to keep going to the end. "Then she left. She didn't even say goodbye and I wasn't invited to the wedding. People had been told that I was her little sister and not her daughter – so it would have been awkward to have me there in case I had said something contrary to that." Catherine sighed.

"It got quieter after she was gone, my grandparents didn't talk to me much and I spent a lot of time in my room with my books. Eve got even more strict with me too, I wasn't allowed to visit friends' houses, or go to parties, and certainly no trips or holidays."

After a moment of companionable silence, Edward noted, "That's why you are so convinced you couldn't have gone to Tynemouth then?"

"Yes – I know that I had never left Edinburgh until I went to university so having a memory from there just doesn't make sense."

Edward put his arm around her and kissed her head, "That must have been pretty lonely?"

Catherine leaned into his shoulder, "It was, but I had my books which became my friends. I got good grades, and - eventually - I got out. I have never looked back since."

Edward stopped and pulled Catherine to him. He kissed her passionately as they stood, the waves splashing at their calves. She felt a need for him, and wanted to get closer still, to become part of him and never feel lonely again.

On the way home they stopped off at an off-licence and bought a couple of bottles of good wine. Catherine had invited him to stay for dinner and she knew that it meant getting more intimate and taking their relationship to a new level, but somehow it didn't seem to faze her. Edward grinned at her impishly when she invited him, and she punched him playfully on the shoulder in response.

They would have the flat to themselves as Liam always went out on a Saturday night anyway - it was his dungeons and dragons gaming night and he wouldn't be home until late the next day.

As they walked across the threshold of the flat Edward had a quick glance around. "This is a nice flat. Very you."

She took the wine and led him into the kitchen, "Thanks … I think!" She was feeling unsure what to say all of a sudden and busied herself making them both something simple to eat. After dinner they sat on the couch and opened the second bottle of wine.

"What will you do about Fiona then?"

"I'll wait," he said. "She'll talk to me when she's ready."

"Typical man!" she teased, breaking the tension that had been built up over the day of serious talk.

Edward looked up and an evil glint shone in his eyes. "You think?" he said as he pounced over and started to tickle her.

The touch of his tickling was electric as she squirmed and wriggled trying to fight off the very welcome physical contact. Then his arms were around her as they lay on the couch together and his hand reached up to touch her face, moving aside a lock of hair.

Catherine looked into his eyes, only inches away, and saw reflected there her own strong emotions. Here was a man who was everything she wanted, strong, confident, intelligent, gentle and sexy. In his eyes she saw the desire, the hunger that she felt returned.

Then he kissed her. Catherine's whole body arched into that kiss, every fibre of her being wanted him and nothing had ever been so 'right'.

The kiss continued as their passion arose. She nuzzled into his embrace. Heart pounding as she lost all sense of time.

His hand stroked her face, her shoulders, her back. Then it slid under her shirt and she felt the deft flick with which he undid her bra. He pulled her shirt up over her head, briefly interrupting the kissing. Then he wrapped himself around her again and put his mouth back on hers. He stroked her bare back as they lay side by side.

Catherine was weightless and giddy. She wanted to crawl inside him and curl up as he kissed her. Then his lips and tongue were on her neck. His hand cupped her breast as his fingers teased her nipple. Her body was moving into him and she was already so turned on. Still with one arm around her, his mouth moved to her breast whilst his hand moved down between her legs rubbing there through her skirt. A moan escaped from her lips as she yearned for more. With intense excitement she felt him move his hand to pull the fabric of her skirt up and then his hand slid down into her pants. As his fingers made contact, she could feel the wetness there and then he moaned – a sound which pushed her over the edge of ecstasy.

Catherine didn't want to wait any longer and pulled him back to kiss him again, however his fingers continued their maddening movements and she couldn't hold onto him. Then he rolled on top of her. She felt him rub against her, so close, but he held off, his kisses reigning down on her and his fingers teasing. She moaned and was close to begging, as she pulled at him. Then he could hold off no longer.

It was over in only a few minutes with both of them climaxing together. She was surprised by the heat of her passion. As they lay there together, it felt that they were part of one body rather than two.

Afterwards they lay on the couch stroking, kissing and revelling the closeness of touch. The smell of him was like a drug and she wanted to breathe him in. They didn't speak for the longest time, as they idled and basked in the moment.

Then Edward tweaked her nose and said, "So do you have a bed or are we staying on the couch all night."

"You tired?"

"Nope, I want to get properly naked and stretch out," he pulled her to her feet and grabbed the two wine glasses.

They made love for the second time in her bed and it was gentle, slow, passionate, exciting, intoxicating, sensual and more. Edward seemed to know every part of her body intimately, and every touch was electric. They climaxed together again and then lay naked and exhausted but still too bound up in each other to sleep.

Edward made love to her a third time that night. Each time more passionate than the last and each time raising her to new heights of ecstasy. More than half-way through the night, they fell asleep in each other's arms.

~ 15 ~

Violation

Merwynn lay awake clutching tightly to the rough blanket at her chest with both hands. The darkness only just held at bay by the low light of the moon filtering through the shuttered widow. She was feeling a dread, not knowing if he was coming that night. He came most nights now and it was not with a gentle touch that he took her.

The silence stretched on painfully as she waited.

Maybe, just maybe, he had tired of it and would leave her alone.

Maybe tonight she would not have to endure him.

Maybe?

As the tiny hope dawned, muscles started to relax and sweet sleep beckoned gratefully, the soft scrape of a footstep could be heard outside her cell. The click of the latch and the door creaked open as she lay with her eyes closed tight. Her grip tightened. Every muscle in her body stiffened in anticipation of what was to come. She tried to ignore the sound, to tell herself it was not happening. However, she couldn't shut out the wafted scent of sour body odour, coal dust and the sharp tang of iron.

Brother Adalbert entered without knocking. He turned and closed the door sliding across the wooden latch which ensured their privacy. It was the same latch she had once used to keep him out, and she had been severely punished for it the next day. Within two steps he was at her bedside. He stood there for a moment before he forcefully pulled the blanket away, tearing away the meagre security she had.

Merwynn's fists clenched on nothing as she held them tightly to her chest.

Without preamble, or tenderness, he pulled her linen shift up to her waist and then stood back up. She heard him hiss through his teeth – a bitter vicious sound filled with contempt and loathing.

Then he lay down on top of her. He fumbled with his own cassock and found purchase against the end of the bed. He pressed roughly into her but found the entrance dry and unyielding. Grunting a curse he spat into his hand and used his fingers to make her painfully accessible.

She wanted to cry out but knew he would punish her for that and bit her lip instead.

Satiated, he got up and pulled his cassock down to cover himself again.

The act over, he would not be as violent as he sometimes was beforehand. If she tried to refuse, which she had done in the early days - or more recently if she spoke at all - the consequences were painful for days.

She opened her eyes a crack, and watched him as he smoothed down his robes. She instinctively started to pull her shift down but froze leaving herself exposed as she caught his glance which held only contempt. Those eyes that had once captivated her now only revolted Merwynn and saw disgust in return. It was clear from that cold hard stare that he considered the sin all hers and hated her for it.

Brother Adalbert left as quietly as he came, leaving her alone and miserable. After the quiet echoes of his footsteps had dissipated, she used a cloth to wipe as much of him away as she could. Then she pulled down her shift and dragged the rough blanket back over her. She turned onto her side and clutched the treacherous covering tightly over her head, pulling her knees up to roll into a ball. She felt the tears leak unbidden out of her eyes but held back the sob which would betray her. There was nowhere she could turn and nothing to be done but endure - to admit the sin was to be turned out. Once again, she thought how even her father's proposed marriage would have been better than this. But maybe this was what she deserved. Maybe this was her punishment for not reaching out to Cwen, and letting that innocent little girl get dragged out of the haystack to her awful fate.

~ 16 ~

Shaken

Catherine jumped awake with a shudder, the duvet gripped tightly in her hands. Still beside her, Edward was shocked awake as well. She was shaking from head to foot.

"What is it?" he asked reaching out to hold her arm.

Catherine recoiled, then turned to look at him lying beside her on the bed. "Oh," she shook her head trying to get the image of the cell out of her mind. "Just a bad dream."

It didn't feel like a dream though, it was more like one of the hypnosis sessions and the images were still very clear in her head. "I'm going to the loo," she started to climb over him in the bed.

Edward caught her, delaying her movement. "Are you okay?"

She smiled weakly. "Yes, I'm fine. I'm not used to having someone in my bed at night."

He gave a broad smiled, "Hmm, I am glad to hear that. We'll have to see what we can do to rectify that!"

She escaped his grasp and he gave he an affectionate pat on her bare bottom as she grabbed her dressing gown. The action grated even though she knew it was not meant as anything other than playful.

Catherine sat on the loo with her head in her hands. She could not shake the acrid smell of the monk from her dream out of her head. She wanted to shower and scrub her skin to get the memory of him off her. The revulsion she'd felt at his touch and the desperate hopelessness of her situation made her feel nauseous.

No, not my situation! It was a dream for goodness' sake! She looked at herself in the mirror and wasn't convinced that she recognised her reflection. *Pull yourself together girl.*

With that she washed her hands and went back to bed.

Catherine and Edward spent the day together and she started to feel comfortable again. Edward put her low mood down to being sleep deprived and said that it was good to know that she had a dark side too. They sat together on the couch watching a movie that she chose, his arm around her and her head on his shoulder. She noticed that throughout the film his thumb rubbed her upper arm.

He'd agreed to meet some mates for a drink that night so left at around four o'clock to get ready. He hugged her for a long time on the doorstep and kissed her. "Get some sleep, I think I have worn you out."

Catherine pushed a smile on her face, "Have a nice night, and no picking up any strange women!"

"Ok, normal ones okay though?" he quipped back with a wink as he went down the communal stairs two at a time.

Catherine was quick to shut the door, grateful to be alone again. She felt rather overwhelmed and a bit suffocated, whilst at the same time being flattered and rather bemused by his attentions. He was well out of her league, and it would only be a matter of time before he realised that.

A little later, Liam arrived home after gaming all night. For some reason he could survive without sleep every Saturday night and not suffer the remotest side effects. He wanted all the gory details and she told him about the dinner and love making.

"What's up?" he asked as he cocked his head to one side.

"Nothing," she shrugged.

Liam continued to give her a tilted stare.

She paused and then caught his expression. "I just had a bad dream last night that's all. It was nothing but it's been bugging me all day."

"What about?"

She hesitated, feeling that the words said out loud would solidify the memory, giving it power somehow.

"I'm not sure ..."

"Come on Catherine, it was a dream, wasn't it?"

"Yes, but it was horrible. I was having sex with a monk ... but I didn't want to be."

"You mean rape?"

"No, that's the problem. He wasn't raping me, I let him do it, I ... didn't fight him off. It was like ... I didn't have a choice to deny him."

Liam raised his eyebrows in a sceptical expression she knew well. "That's still rape." He said flatly. Then he got a twinkle in his eye and added. "Do you think it was guilt – after all you were committing a sin having sex with Edward. Your grandmother's Christian upbringing seeping through?"

Liam was laughing at her and although she knew that he was being funny and she had no real right to be annoyed, she was very put out. She wanted to rationalise the experience but couldn't grasp why a dream had so distressed her. She grunted at Liam and went to make herself a hot chocolate.

Whilst there she made herself a hot water bottle and went to bed early. She curled around the bottle and huddled up in bed. She should be feeling loved up and happy, but in truth she felt rather lonely and cut off.

Catherine fell asleep and the same dream haunted her all that night. She would awake sobbing having experienced the same treatment again. Each dream was the same, but also had subtle differences - a different light, a different season and smell to the air. The monk changed, he aged, and he became harder and more violent towards her. No matter how quiet or still she was, he would find some excuse to hit her.

When dawn finally came, Catherine didn't want to sleep any more. She was exhausted but didn't want to go through the horrors again. She pulled on a dressing gown and got up. Standing at the kitchen sink she shivered and wrapped the robe around her tightly.

She went through to the living room and sat on the couch with a glass of water and pulled a blanket over her shoulders. Liam had left his tobacco on the table and for the first time in two years she rolled herself a cigarette and sat there smoking it. It tasted horrible but brought her back to the present day, banishing the dream residue.

The next few hours seemed to last forever as she sat doing nothing, almost in a vegetative state. She didn't want to go back to sleep, knowing that it would take her back to the monk. She pulled herself together and went and made a strong cup of coffee and then had a shower. She had a full day of work to get through and had to snap out of it.

Work helped and forced her back into the mundane tasks of the present day. There were client meetings to be held and marketing reports to submit, and all of it took concentration – another couple of cups of strong coffee helped. She was exhausted but as the day progressed, she started to feel better and by afternoon she had managed to shake the feelings that hung onto the edges of her consciousness.

She got a text from Edward in the afternoon. It said, "Can't get you off my mind after Saturday night X"

She smiled and texted back, "Well, we'll have to do it again sometime. Tuesday Ceroc?"

"Of course. See you there. X"

~ 17 ~

New Year

For the next few weeks, things seemed to cruise. The dreams continued however, becoming more persistent. The hypnosis sessions mirrored the same experiences but often with more clarity and detail. There were images that she gleaned from the night-time ventures into her own subconscious which stunned her in their complexity. Like the feelings and impressions of the place she had lived in.

Edward continued to worry about Fiona, and Catherine again offered to see if she needed a female ear, so he arranged for the three of them to meet up for a coffee.

When Fiona arrived at the book shop cafe, Catherine was struck by how different she seemed from the tall and confident woman she had met at the party only a few months before. She was looking rather hesitant and nervous. Her hair seemed duller and unkempt, tied back in a low ponytail, and she was wearing far less make-up. Edward ordered them all coffees and they chatted about very mundane things. Then Edward made an excuse and went off to browse the books.

"Is everything okay with you Fiona?"

"What do you mean?" she looked up at Catherine, a sharp edge to her voice.

"Edward's worried about you. You just don't seem yourself."

"Oh," she said as her shoulders slumped. "It's nothing, Ed's a fusspot." She seemed to want to leave it there, but Catherine let the silence wash over them - as she had learnt to do from Bastian - and Fiona gathered her thoughts then continued.

"You know that Rick and I have split up?"

"Yes."

"It wasn't his fault at all. He tried so hard to make things work but he wasn't right for me. I can't even tell you what was wrong. He just wasn't my soulmate ..." her voice faded to a whisper. Then she discreetly locked eyes with Catherine and asked, "Do you believe in past lives?"

"I'm not sure ... I may be starting to."

"I do. And it's beginning to make sense why I was so frightened of knives before." She leaned in closer, "Don't tell Edward this because he wouldn't understand, but I was murdered. By a husband whom I adored. There wasn't even any reason for it, nothing I could understand anyway." She laughed at Catherine's shocked expression. "I keep going over it again and again. Trying to work out what I'd done wrong ... why he did it. Bastian and I have revisited it so many times but we can't get anything more. It is so vivid. I was sitting at a dressing table taking off my long white gloves, smiling at myself in the mirror. We had just come back from a fun party and I was daydreaming about making love to him again. I was so happy and so in love. Then he came up behind me. He tenderly put a hand on my shoulder and then I saw the knife in his other clenched fist. He smiled, Catherine. I wasn't scared because it was the same warm loving expression that I knew so well. Then he plunged the knife into my heart – smiling all the time." Fiona held her hand to her chest as if stemming the flow of blood. "I can still feel the pain, but it is the betrayal and confusion I feel most keenly."

Fiona stopped for a moment and took a breath. She tucked a stray strand of hair behind her ear and took a sip of coffee.

Catherine waited, not sure what to say.

"Anyway," Fiona continued, stirring her coffee for no good reason, "It's made me realise that I don't want to repeat the same pattern again. I've spent my whole adult life trying to live up to my parents' relationship. Trying to find that soulmate like mum and dad were. Trying to be the perfect woman so I can find the perfect man. Always so careful about how I looked and presenting myself for others rather than for myself. It's made me realise that I've been bending over backwards to be what other people want. But what if I find that soulmate and he is an abuser? What if that perfect lover is just going to kill me again."

"That seems a lot to go through," Catherine could see why Edward was worried. Fiona seemed to be talking in circles but also seemed to be trying to work through it. "So what are you going to do now?"

"I want to find myself again, to strip away the façade that I have put up for so long. I think I need to be by myself for a while. Find my footing again. Can you understand that? I need to be the one in control and not have to make decisions based on what other people want."

"Yes, I think we all have to find ourselves sometimes. Just know that Edward is worried about you. He loves you."

"I know he does," Fiona sighed, "but I have to do this for myself."

Edward appeared again with a couple of books he had bought and the conversation changed entirely.

When it was time to leave, and as soon as they were out of Fiona's earshot, Edward asked what his sister had said.

Catherine reassured him that she was trying to find herself. As requested, she didn't tell him about what Fiona had said about her past life. It was private and inwardly she agreed that Edward probably wouldn't understand.

The festive season wrapped Edinburgh in a magical atmosphere, and with Edward's presence, it felt even more enchanting for Catherine. They spent Christmas together, each moment laced with laughter and tenderness. Edward had a way of making even the simplest activities – like decorating the Christmas tree – feel special. They would often pause, finding themselves lost in conversation or laughter, and Catherine cherished how natural and right it seemed to be with him.

Their gift exchange was a heartfelt affair. Catherine unwrapped a beautifully bound copy of her favourite book from Edward, a thoughtful gesture that showed how well he knew her. In return, she gave him a vintage compass, symbolizing the journey they were on together. The significance wasn't lost on either of them, and Edward's warm smile filled Catherine with a sense of belonging.

Mistletoe hung in the doorway, and they found themselves gravitating towards it often, sharing kisses that were both playful and profound. Each gentle touch and shared glance under the mistletoe deepened Catherine's sense of connection and security in their relationship.

As they welcomed the New Year amidst the bustling crowds on Princess Street, the world around them faded into a blur. Surrounded by over 350,000 people, they created a cocoon of intimacy, holding each other close, ensuring they wouldn't be separated. To Catherine, the throngs of partygoers melted away, leaving only her and Edward, their eyes locked in a shared moment of hope and promise for the future.

Throughout the holidays, Catherine's recurring nightmare persisted, yet its grip on her seemed to loosen. Edward's presence in her life brought a new perspective, a comforting counterbalance to the unsettling dreams. She began to view the nightmares as a mere part of her existence, something to acknowledge and then set aside as she embraced each new day with Edward. This acceptance marked a subtle yet significant shift in her approach to life, hinting at a newfound resilience and optimism.

After the holidays, work started again and they were back at Ceroc. Edward was dancing, whirling around flirtatiously with an excellent dancer whose full skirt flew through the air in wide circles. Catherine reminded herself again that she should find a skirt like that to wear. Edward was enjoying himself and the girl flushed with excitement and exhilaration. It was like watching poetry in motion and she was proud that her boyfriend was so skilled at dancing.

Then she felt a tentative tap on her shoulder.

"Hi," said a blond, blue-eyed angelic looking girl.

Catherine was sure that she recognised her but couldn't place where from.

"He's a good dancer, isn't he?" She said in a flat voice.

"Yeah, he is."

"My name's Shona," she said holding out her hand.

"Hi," Catherine was feeling rather strange but shook her hand anyway. It somehow didn't seem the appropriate greeting for the dance club.

"Look, I don't mean to be rude but ... well, you're going out with Edward, aren't you." It wasn't a question.

"Yes, though I'm not sure ..."

"Please," Shona interrupted, with hand raised, "hear me out."

Catherine paused then nodded, though her now ever-present smile had vanished.

"He's not what he seems. I went out with him for several months and at the start it was wonderful, but then he started to ..." Shona stopped mid-sentence.

Catherine could feel the anger rising in her from the pit of her stomach and through her chest. She crossed her arms. "Started to what? You might as well finish."

"You don't understand ... I'm trying to help you."

"No, you are trying to bad-mouth someone. I remember you now, that first night I came to Ceroc. You were in the bar making eyes at Edward."

"Yes, but ..."

"No," Catherine said putting her hand up between them, "on second thoughts, I don't want to hear it."

Edward came hurrying up looking worried. "What's going on?"

Cahterine heard an edge to his voice she had not heard before.

"Nothing," Catherine took his hand, "let's dance," and she led him back to the dance floor.

Shona stood there with the same look on her face as she had in the bar, blank and unreadable.

Catherine said nothing to Edward as they danced, but the incident went round and round in her head as she swayed her annoyance out to the last song of the night. She wanted to know what it was all about but didn't want to ask Edward directly. If an explanation was coming, it had to come from him.

When the song finished, they declined the invitation to go for a drink with the others and got into Catherine's car to go home.

As soon as Edward had buckled his seatbelt, he broached the subject. "What did Shona want?" he asked in a voice that seemed strained.

"To warn me against you," Catherine kept her voice bland.

"That bitch." He said it with more vehemence than she had ever heard in his voice before.

She turned to look at him, eyebrows raised, but said nothing.

"Sorry," he said, "it's just she's been making my life difficult for some time."

Catherine waited for more as he paused awkwardly. "Are you going to tell me?"

"It's embarrassing," he sighed. "How much did she tell you?"

"Why don't you start at the beginning and tell me your side of the story."

"Okay," he said, "but let's get back to your place first."

Catherine started the car and they drove home in silence, all the way she felt a lump of lead in her stomach. When they got home Edward helped himself to a stiff whiskey and gave her one, then sat down beside her on the couch nursing the drink like it was a lifeline.

"Where do I start?" he said.

Catherine remained silent and let him think.

"I met Shona about three years ago, through a rock-climbing club I belonged to then. We went out for about eight months and I must admit that I fell for her quite hard." He looked at Catherine nervously, and then added, "It was short lived though."

"Go on?" She felt something horrible was coming.

"Well, it ended rather abruptly one night when I found her in bed with my flatmate."

"What?" Catherine was shocked, not only that a girlfriend would do that, but more so that a flatmate would betray him in that way.

"We'd been out on the town and had had way too much to drink. Then we came home and fell into bed and I fell fast asleep. I don't know what it was that woke me but when I did, she wasn't there and the bed was cold. So I went looking for her. That's when I heard the two of them 'at it' from the next room."

"What did you do?"

"I banged on the door and told her to come out, which she did. She tried to tell me that she'd gone to the loo and gone back to the wrong room, that she was too drunk and didn't realise it wasn't me. All bullshit of course."

"What about the flatmate?"

"I gave him notice to move out the next morning. Didn't want to live with him after that."

"I'm not surprised," Catherine was feeling very sorry for Edward now, "that must have been horrible."

"Yes, but that was only the start."

"What do you mean?"

"She started to hang around wherever I went. It took my friends a long time to know what was going on because she kept 'bumping' into them and saying we were back together. When I tried to nip that in the bud, she told me that she was pregnant."

"Was the pregnancy real?"

"No. I found out a few weeks later that it was all a hoax. Then she accused me of being unfaithful to her in front of my new girlfriend, and ... well it ruined that relationship. So I cut ties. I had to change my numbers. I stopped going rock-climbing because she was always there. I even left town for a few months – took a contract abroad. Thing is, she hasn't caused trouble for over a year now and I thought she'd backed off. I thought it was all over. Even when she started coming to Ceroc occasionally, she seemed to hover in the background. I should have known that she was going to cause drama again."

Catherine put her hand on his shoulder and rubbed it. She felt for him but knew nothing she could say to help.

Turning to look at her straight in the eyes he said, "I promise you, I was never unfaithful."

His eyes were pleading as Catherine looked deep into them. She could see no hint of deception there however hard she looked.

"Catherine?"

"Yes"

"You do believe me, don't you?"

"Of course I do," she wrapped her arms about him, but deep, deep down, a seed of doubt had been sown.

~ 18 ~
The Feast

Merwynn had never been passionate about the church, not like her father, but she had believed that God answered Hilda's prayers when he turned the snakes to stone. He did help the deserving. She might not be the most pious of his servants but how could he leave her to suffer like this? Over time she learnt to hate the deity who watched over her pain and suffering in such silence - condoning Brother Adalbert by inaction. She had prayed to God to strike Adalbert down, or to intercede in some way - but her maker had maintained a steadfast silence.

Although less often now, Adalbert still came whenever he wanted and, even when he didn't appear, she spent the nights waiting in fear of him. Her stomach in knots and too tense to sleep more than a few snatched exhausted minutes at a time. Always on alert for any noise, footstep or touch of the door. Always wide awake at a moment's notice.

The anticipation was almost worse than the bruises - the moments of hope that 'maybe' he would leave her alone. Having once felt giddy with life, Merwynn was now trapped and isolated. Even the other nuns started to shun her. Maybe they knew what was going on and, if so, chose to do nothing to help her. Maybe she was a sacrificial lamb who the other nuns had left to her fate, relieved that it was not them. Then again, maybe they were reacting to her withdrawing into herself. She could not bear to see the same expression on the nuns' faces that she had seen so often on Adalbert's. That shame added to the guilt she already carried around, and she was suffocating under the weight of it all.

Then a seedling of an idea began to grow. If salvation was to come it would not be by divine intervention nor could anyone in the monastery come to her aid. She would have to do something about it herself.

One day an opportunity presented itself when an ealdorman and his retinue arrived at Streoneshalch. A few days beforehand the monastery was given warning that a feast was expected to be held in their honour and the residents went into frantic activity to pull out all the stops. Three long tables were set out, two along the outer walls and one across the shorter end of the long hall. The nuns set about baking bread and butchering the meat to hang before being roasted. It was all hands to the ready.

Then the retinue arrived and the monastery was full of noise and activity. Merwynn watched cautiously from behind a door which had been left ajar, fascinated by the new arrivals in the long hall. Burly men who were talking together in gruff voices and banging their fists on the table whilst they laughed at each other's stories. These men were very different to those she had known as a child, or the monks that she lived with. Their clothes were richly embroidered, their hair cut and fashioned, even their bearing was different to those she had seen before. In her youth and as the daughter of a thegn, Merwynn had been the top of her social class. These ealdormen were second only to the king and were served by thegns, it humbled Merwynn to even be in their presence. At the top table sat a tall thin man stiff backed, and dressed in elegant rich clothes - either side of him were two younger men. One about the same age as Merwynn and one a couple of years younger – all clean shaven, washed and brushed as if for a wedding. Merwynn couldn't tear her eyes away.

The sights and sounds were rich and thick but it was the smell of the feast that was most intoxicating. The heavy rich smell of venison and hare filled the air, along with roast duck and goose, making Merwynn's stomach groan. Their usual staple vegetable broth was nothing like this.

Another younger nun joined Merwynn by the door and giggled as she watched the men. Then they both jumped as a clapped rebuke made them turn around to see the abbess standing behind them.

Merwynn froze and dropped her eyes. The younger nun was still too excited to notice the reprimand and whispered, "Who are these people?"

"They are the Kings men - the ealdorman, his sons and their bodyguard. The high born of the kingdom."

"Why are they here though?"

"This is the house of God. They are here, child, because it is their right to be here. They are resting on their way north and it is our duty to serve them." The nun handed Merwynn and the other girl pitchers of wine with a gesture that told them not to ask any more questions, and she pointed Merwynn towards the top table.

Whilst Merwynn was pouring a cup for the younger of the three men sitting at the centre of the top table, her seedling idea burst into flower. She deliberately spilt the dark red liquid in his lap. Then, before he even had time to react, she crouched down to delicately dab at his upper thigh with her serving cloth, her words filled with breathless apology, saying, "Forgive me my lord."

She raised her eyes and caught his gaze as she looked up into his young but already scarred face, her hand pausing on his leg. His lust was instantly recognisable. Her plan could work.

This man, Hengist, was the key to saving her. If she could find a provider, she could leave it all behind, Adalbert, the stone prison of the monastery, and God. She knew that she was beyond marriage now, she had no dowry to provide a good match anyway, but if she could find a lover that would provide for her, then maybe escape was possible.

The ealdorman's son was not unattractive. He had the gangly arms and legs of a man not yet fully developed but the broad shoulders and muscular body of one trained in the sword from an early age. He had dark hair and thick eyebrows, with blue eyes which were attractive enough to detract from his very broken nose and scarred cheek. His hair was cut short, and even, all around his head, and it appeared he had taken time to comb it through – it was a new style which must have come from the royal court. The eyes though were gentle in comparison; they didn't have the hard glint that Adalbert's did.

She was still touching the man's leg and he put his hand over hers sliding it further up almost to his groin. She pulled her hand away and lowered her eyes for a moment.

"I will pray for you tonight," she tried to sound sultry, the way her father's women had when they'd wanted something. She glanced up at him again to register the one-sided smile on his face and the twinkle in his eyes. He had understood the meaning. This man could change her destiny – and free her from misery – but not just by praying for him.

When the feast was over, the men slept in the hall and on makeshift mattresses. Most of the monks and nuns went back to their cells for the few hours rest before the bells would once again peel.

Merwynn waited at the chapel, kneeling in prayer at the altar. This was all or nothing. If Adalbert went to her room and found her missing, she knew the consequences would be dire – she hoped that he would not risk creaking through the corridors with so many visitors in the monastery. For once she

125

wanted to hear the scrape of the door opening – the chapel door this time - but when it did, she had to swallow hard.

She heard Hengist entering and closing the chapel door, and with a knot of anxiety in the pit of her stomach, she listened to his lopsided gait as he walked up and knelt to cross himself beside her. It was not the angry step of Adalbert. The young man prayed for a moment head bowed and hands clasped showing her that he was a believer and, she hoped, a man of honour.

"Are you praying for me?" He asked.

"I am praying for us both."

His hands held in prayer parted, and the one nearest to her came to rest on Merwynn's shoulder. "Will you take pity on a poor soldier?"

She couldn't speak as his hand caressed her shoulder and slid down to the small of her back. She seemed frozen on the spot and stayed motionless as if still praying. Even when he turned to face her, she still didn't move or respond. His other hand crossed in front of Merwynn as he pulled her around to face him still on his knees. She looked straight into his face for the first time as he looked directly into her eyes.

Lifting her to her feet, she stood there mutely in front of the kneeling lord who looked up at her with a deep expression in his eyes. Their eyes locked together.

"Why so sad my lady?" he asked.

She could feel the tears welling up and rolling down her face but was not aware of crying. His hands ran up her legs pulling the robes up with them till he passed her knees. As they got higher, he slowed – she was not stopping him but the silent tears increased in intensity as she continued to look at him.

His face revealed confusion and it made him look at her in a different way. With his hands still on her bare legs he stopped, held motionless for a moment. She could see it all written on his face; he knew that her sorrow was more than a show of guilt. She saw indecision in his eyes, a hesitation. He would think that she didn't want this and in a moment he would walk away.

She had to overcome this, the revulsion of being touched. This was her only chance. Now or never.

When he started to take his hands away and she could feel him pull back - in that moment, when he didn't push her through it - she knew what she wanted. The force that held her immobile evaporated and Merwynn leaned forward catching his hands in her own. Putting them back onto her legs.

After a moment of hesitation he grasped at her thighs with increased intensity. He pushed her robes up further and holding them aloft he started to kiss her thighs, his rough hands holding her buttocks as he worked his way further up and his tongue found the place between her legs.

The sensation was shocking, the coiled tension in her body started to unravel and she could feel the room tilting backwards, her body turned to jelly as her legs started to shake. Merwynn thought that she couldn't stand any more but he continued, his hands pulling her against his face. Then the tension in her abdomen grew almost unbearable and waves of pleasure washed over her, leaving her quivering and spent. She had never felt anything like it before. Then her legs collapsed under her and she fell into his waiting arms.

Then he laid her down on the floor of the chapel with one arm under her shoulders whilst the other still rubbed between her legs. A moan escape from her lips as he leant over and put his lips on her mouth with a long lingering passionate, kiss. He pulled her robes up further and her legs parted of their own volition. He pulled at his own leg garments releasing the knot that held them in place.

Her body craved his; she needed him inside of her, wanted to be part of him. This stranger, this young man who seemed to know her body better than she did.

Still kissing he rolled on top of her and then paused. She could feel the push of his organ between her legs but he held back. One final time he pulled away and looked into her face.

The pause was unbearable to her. She wanted this, she wanted him right then. She pulled his head back to kiss her again and then her hands rolled down his back to his buttocks as she tried to pull him into her. He resisted for a moment then released and slid into her welcome embrace. The tension arched her body and curled her toes. It built with each thrust until the sensation exploded, pulsing through her body with release. Her head was full of lights and tingling as her whole body writhed in ecstasy. She was weightless like she was falling from a great height. Red hot she juddered over and over again. It lasted for an age until she felt that she could bear no more as he pushed, faster and faster until the sweat was pouring off him and he convulsed.

They both lay breathless and exhausted on the floor of the chapel, Merwynn surprised by the sensations he had awoken in her. She reminded herself how she'd felt when first she laid with Adalbert. This time she would not be swept away and would stay in control. However nice he might be now, she knew only too well how fast that could change. She expected him to get up and leave immediately but to her surprise the man continued to hold her, continued to kiss and stroke her although he was already spent.

The affection was strange to her and knocked her a little off balance. She followed his lead though and reminded herself that she needed this man to want her, to need her. He was her only chance of escape.

~ 19 ~

People Watching

Catherine spotted Shona the next time they went to Ceroc. Edward stuck close to her though and refrained from dancing, giving his admirers the excuse that he wasn't feeling up to it that night.

It was reassuring that Edward was showing Shona that he was 'with' Catherine now. Catherine suppressed the urge to walk up to her and tear her hair out. Who did Shona think she was, coming into their world to ruin a perfectly good evening.

Catherine could see the poisoned dwarf over the other side of the room scowling at Edward and looking at Catherine with appearing pity – and it made her blood boil. How dare she!

Then another girl and a friend of Edward's came over to them, freshly off the dance floor and still panting.

"Come on Edward," the girl said tugging on his sleeve, "I've worn Graham out. Your turn to come dance." It wasn't a question and she was not giving him an option to say no, so with an apologetic glance towards Catherine - and reciprocal shrug - Edward went off to dance with the girl leaving Graham sitting exhausted beside her.

"I see Shona's back then," said Graham.

"You know her?"

"God yes," he took a large gulp of water and wiped the sweat from his forehead with his sleeve. "She's the psycho bitch from Hell."

"Not your favourite person then."

He laughed, relaxing a little, then turned more serious. "She got her claws into Edward a while back and wouldn't let go. She's a manipulative lying cow. I assume Edward's told you about her?"

Catherine got the feeling that Edward had already told him that she knew. In fact she got the distinct feeling that he'd been asked to come over and verify the situation for her.

"Yes, he has."

"Well, you know all about it then. She's unbelievable. She even attacked one of his girlfriends, did he tell you that?"

"No, he left that part out."

"Hmm, I thought not. He felt pretty bad about that. The girl was put in hospital but didn't press charges because she was so scared of Shona. The girl ended the relationship with Edward though. Simply couldn't handle it any more. Edward was really cut up about it."

"I'm not surprised," she looked out and watched Edward dance, whilst his friend continued. He was smiling but he also looked less relaxed than normal.

"I didn't see him for about six months after that. He's a proud man. Not something he'd probably volunteer – especially to the new love of his life." He said playfully.

She smiled and punched him playfully on the arm.

When Edward came back Catherine wrapped her arms about him and hugged him close, like she never wanted to let him go.

Catherine decided that she would ignore Shona and avoid her altogether. Shona might have been violent to another girl but Catherine was considerably bigger than her and refused to be afraid. After all she knew how to handle herself.

About an hour later she went to the ladies and when she came out of the cubicle her whole body froze. Shona was there. She stood facing the mirror with her back toward Catherine.

"I need to talk to you," Shona said looking at Catherine's reflection whilst she fiddled with her lipstick, making imaginary touches to the already perfect paint job. She was a pretty girl, with the perfect blue eyes and the long blond curly hair, the petite body with all the right curves. She looked too good to be real. Catherine could have hated her just for that.

Catherine gritted her teeth and went to the sink to wash her hands. She tried her best to ignore the smaller woman. Catherine loathed confrontations no matter how much Shona's presence made her blood boil.

"We really do need to talk," Shona said again in a flat tone.

"I am not interested in what you have to say," Catherine blurted out a little too quickly, to cover the stress she was feeling at being cornered.

"Oh. I see. He's done it again. He's manipulative and dangerous Catherine. You have to be careful. You have no idea."

"No, you've no idea," she turned to face Shona head on, not liking the mirrored conversation. "You are the one who needs help Shona! Psychiatric help!"

Shona put her lipstick away in her purse and turned to face Catherine as well. "Do you know that he put his last girlfriend in the hospital?" She sounded genuinely desperate.

Their eyes locked together. "No, Shona that was you!" Catherine's voice escalated, both in pitch and intensity, yet it carried the risky thrill of bating a tiger, brimming with a daring challenge.

Shona looked like she had been slapped and it seemed to stop her in her tracks.

After a few moments Shona looked down and said, "Clever, very clever," then looking back at Catherine she added, "but then why was it that HE went to jail for it?" With that she turned on her heel and walked out of the bathroom.

Now Catherine was confused. The seed had sprouted an invisible thread of root which dug into her subconscious as she struggled to dismiss Shona's vindictive words.

No, she was as mean and manipulative as Edward had said she was. Poison. Catherine decided that she would not swallow her lies.

She didn't tell Edward what had happened in the toilets because it would upset him. She went back and tried to enjoy the evening. Shona was nowhere to be seen but she could feel her malevolent presence in the room wherever she went. After another half hour she gave up and called it a night, pleading an early work start in the morning. Edward was going out for a drink with Graham so they arranged to see each other later in the week.

When she got home, much to her annoyance, Liam was there with Jojo. Unable to wait until they were alone Catherine told Liam what had happened with Shona.

"Sounds like she's totally off her rocker!" Liam said between puffs of his joint.

It did not surprise Catherine that Jojo had a different take on the subject though.

"Not necessarily," Jojo said refusing the joint from Liam. "Maybe his friends just believe Edward because of what he's told them. You said that Edward's friend didn't see him for months after the girl was beaten up. Where did he go? Maybe he WAS in jail?"

"Unlikely," said Liam, "don't you think his friends would have known if he was in jail?"

"It all depends on how well they know him. He may well have told people he was visiting family or something. I know one man who told his daughter he was at university for three years although he was in jail for fraud."

"Slightly different," Catherine said with a touch of sarcasm.

"Is it?" Jojo said, sounding like a genuine question rather than the barbed comment that Catherine was sure it was meant to be.

Catherine stared daggers at her but had no answer.

"You can't take what anyone says on face value because you don't know," Jojo said, as if she was teaching a lesson. "Just because you're emotionally involved with Edward doesn't make him right and her wrong."

Liam butted in as he passed Catherine the joint. "Well, I've met the guy and he seems pretty solid to me."

"That doesn't mean anything," Jojo poured herself a glass of wine. She held the glass up and looked at swirling around and then took a sip.

Catherine wanted to take the opportunity to say something but her mind had gone blank.

Then Jojo was talking again in that matter-of-fact tone which made Catherine's teeth itch. "One thing is certain though, one of them is lying. And whoever it is, has already proved they are also dangerous. Probably psychopathic."

"Bit extreme," Catherine found her voice again.

Jojo rounded on her, "Not if you'd seen the people I've seen at the 'wellness centre' and known the things they've done – things you wouldn't imagine one human being could do to another," Jojo shivered.

"Like what?" Catherine asked.

Jojo shook her head.

"Go on," said Liam. "Like what?"

"Okay, well without giving you names. One boy has been in the psych ward for years. When asked why he held his little sister's head under the bath water, long after she had stopped struggling, said, 'because she wanted to ride my bicycle'. Then there was ..."

"Okay, okay, I get it," said Liam not wanting any more.

"But why would anyone do that?" Catherine could not comprehend anyone being so callous.

Jojo looked into her eyes and said, "Because they can. Some people are born without any empathy. They don't care about anyone else ... and there are far more of them than you'd think!"

Catherine could not fathom a human being who had no emotion, no conscience or remorse. She knew there were nasty people out there but really? To be born without any human feeling towards their fellow man? Liam seemed to agree with her.

Catherine's temples throbbed and she couldn't take in any more. She let their voices fade inside her head as they debated back and forth, Liam talking about human nature and Jojo talking science.

Catherine took herself off to bed feeling drained and shaky.

~ 20 ~

The Lover

Merwynn could smell Hengist on her and could still feel the shivers of sexual ecstasy all the next day. That evening she was serving the ealdorman and his sons at the table again, and she could feel Hengist's eyes follow her about the room. When she reached out to take his plate his hand stroked the back of her thigh. She felt a thrill of excitement and yearning burn through her, at the same time her face reddened even though she knew that no-one could have seen the action.

She needed to keep her head if she wanted this plan to work. She needed to be in control.

That night his arms were around her again – this time in his comfortable guest rooms – and in a shared bed. His hands were rough but his touch was gentle and he seemed to relish in her company. They had just finished coupling and he was holding her whilst they both shivered in shared excitement. She didn't want to leave but she knew she could not stay where she was. Things were going well though and she had a smile on her face as she started to dress.

"We continue north tomorrow," he said.

Her face fell as her eyes filled with tears. It was not enough time.

"I would take you with me if I could," he said lifting her chin and wiping away a tear, "but my father would never allow it. He disapproves of women camp followers, for me at least."

She said nothing and continued to pull more clothes on.

"My father has already made a match for me, and I am expected to marry after we have beaten back the enemy. I don't know how long that'll be. The heathen have invaded Northumberland. Our north-most territories are being sacked and burnt and we gather the fyrd to beat them back."

She knew what he referred to, the blue painted Picts had a new king, a Gael of all things, who had raised an army from the bands of savages that inhabited the countries north of Northumberland.

He went on, "With the Viking raids up and down the coast it may be years before I marry. But in the meantime my father expects me to fight and learn to command the fyrd."

Catherine could spit. The fyrd, which had never been called to reclaim Cwen, never called to help the ordinary people when they lost everything. The call to arms by the King, ensuring each lord who had serfs and slaves at their command were duty bound to come, armed with whatever they had – staff, axe, spear or pitch fork. That was the fyrd. It was the might of men of the kingdom and it meant that the harvest could be delayed or worked by the women on top of everything else. It meant hardship and death for many, regardless of the outcome. Now the fyrd, which had never been there to help her, was going to take away her only means of escape. It meant her plan was thwarted and she would once again be at the mercy of Adalbert.

His words also brought back unwelcome memories of Viking violence. Maybe that was why she had been so reckless when she had come to the monastery.

She felt torn apart now, lost in her memories of the attack as Hengist told her of their imminent departure. Brother Adalbert had left her alone whilst the ealdorman's party had been present but now the walls that had once kept her safe would become her prison again.

She got up to leave him with tears streaming down her face. There was nothing to say.

Hengist was confused and asked her to stay.

She shrugged him off and moved away a pace. She straightened her robes and then turned. "I would go with you, if you wanted me."

"Only if you can change your sex, my father will not allow me to take a woman."

"But you want me with you?"

He hesitated. "Yes. Yes, I do," he seemed surprised by his own response.

It was little consolation, but it did ease the pain of leaving. She went back the way she had come, out of his chamber and back towards her own cell. She was deep in thought and didn't notice that her door was slightly ajar. Merwynn missed the figure standing in the corner of her cell. His cowled face hidden in the dark. She went into her cell unprepared for what was to come, taking off her cloak and throwing it on the bed.

As Merwynn began to shed her outer robes, she found herself ensnared in the fabric. It was in this vulnerable state that the first blow struck, a forceful punch to her chest that sent her reeling backward onto the bed. The impact expelled the air from her lungs with such violence that an intense heat surged to her face, accompanied by a wave of paralysing fear. The metallic taste of blood filled her mouth as she gasped desperately for air, struggling to recover from the unexpected assault.

With heart pounding Merwynn knew it was Brother Adalbert – and she knew more was coming.

She struggled out of the robes in a rush, trying to right herself, but as she pulled up another blow fell. This time a kick to her groin. She cried out in pain as she doubled over and felt his hands grabbing for her, pressing over the robes covering her mouth.

"No! You don't make no sound," he growled in her ear.

She muffled a whimper and put her hands up trying to calm him, and he backed off a little. She frantically righted her robes and finally could see her attacker. He had the look of a demented man, his mouth was twisted and his eyes burned with fury.

"I know where you've been. You are a whore. You've poisoned my soul with foul temptations. Now you're poisoning others as well." He spat the words at her as she cowered beneath him.

Merwynn bit her lip and shivered violently. Pleading with her eyes and shaking her head. She racked her brain for an escape, for any action that might end this ordeal, but realised that anything she said would only further enrage him.

He would kill her now, and she would welcome death rather than live like this anymore. He raised his fist again and, with horror, she saw it swing towards the side of her head.

~ 21 ~

Pain

In the morning Catherine's whole body hurt like she had been in a car crash and she groaned with every small movement. The right side of her head throbbed with a pounding headache. Her chest, stomach and lower back ached and the agony radiated out to her arms and legs as well.

She couldn't move without pain, but after a few minutes she inched her way over to the bedside cabinet to find the hangover painkillers and took three straight away. She then lay back and tried to stay as still as possible. Hoping the pain would fade soon.

She lay there for nearly an hour lost in the physical and emotional agony of it all. Even breathing was a torture which had to be endured. When the pills started to take the edge off, she picked up her phone and called into work sick. She was never ill, and she felt guilty calling in. Her boss understood though, and even gave her suggested flu remedies.

Maybe that was it, she thought for a brief moment, maybe she had flu and that was why she was feeling so rotten. Indeed maybe it was because she had been in pain from the flu that she had dream about being beaten up. She tried to tell herself that, but in truth she knew it was the other way around. How could she tell anyone that though, they would think she was crazy?

She had to make an appointment to see Bastian, he would understand. He was the only one who would.

When the painkillers had taken full effect, she rang to try and talk to Bastian, but he was busy. She had another appointment with him a few days later, so maybe she would leave it and talk to him then.

She messaged Edward saying that she wasn't well and was staying off work and would text him when she was feeling better.

She knew that she should sleep but was afraid of what would happen when she did. After a while the pain killers took more effect and lulled her back into the abyss.

~ 22 ~

Maketh the Man

Merwynn came around on the floor of her cell, alone. The side of her head throbbing painfully as she reached up to feel some matted blood in her hair. The light of early dawn was at her window and the birds of the forest, were in song already. Brother Adalbert was gone, though she had no memory of him leaving. Her whole body ached and she felt stabs of pain in her chest whenever she moved. She was surprised to find that she was not dead.

Then with clarity of mind, she knew she had to get out of there, she could not stay another minute. Brother Adalbert hadn't killed her, but it had likely been his intention. She had to leave, and her only chance was to leave with Hengist.

Pulling herself up onto the cot she winced in pain. She had to get to the other side of the monastery. The fyrd was leaving at dawn and she might already be too late. She reached painfully for the cloak which she had discarded only hours before and pulled it towards her, holding it to her chest. Then she moaned as she pushed herself to her feet. The room spun and she nearly fell backwards. She held a hand against the wall to steady herself and breathed painfully. She shifted one foot forwards, and then the other. Every tiny movement was like a dagger in her chest, hips and groin and she could feel bones moving in the side of her chest where they shouldn't.

Gritting her teeth she paused and bent down painfully to reach under her cot. She pulled out the small, wrapped bundle and opened it. Inside was the coiled stone snake and the silver ring. She resisted the urge to throw the ring across the room. It had value and may be of use. She slipped it and the snake into her pocket and took one last glance at her cell before turning her back on it.

She shuffled through the quiet corridors as fast as her broken body would allow her. As long as the morning bells had not rung yet she might be in time. Hengist had said that he was not allowed to take a woman with him - but still he wanted her. There had to be a way, he could not leave her behind to be murdered. Anything had to be better than that – even going to war. She was leaving this place behind her and each step took her closer to salvation. If she could not go with her lord as a woman, then she would go with him as a man.

~ 23 ~

Warning Bells

Catherine couldn't identify the sound nor was she even aware of waking up. It wasn't bird song, nor the sound of water. It was like a lot of persistent tiny bells. The sound kept changing and still she could not remember what it meant.

She had been concentrating so hard in her dream on blocking out the pain, that it took an age to wake up fully. She was disorientated and confused by the colours and sounds around her – not to mention the chemical smells that hit her when she came to.

It was overwhelming and she shook her head trying to comprehend where she was. Then it clicked into place. Her phone was ringing. The colours were her familiar bedroom and the smells were the soap powders on the sheets and pyjamas, the shampoo smell of her hair and yesterday's shower gel on her skin.

Smell was the one sense that she rarely used. Now she found it overwhelmed by the acrid chemical onslaught and she wretched as she struggled out of bed. Luckily the pain had subsided somewhat and moving was easier. Putting her hand over her mouth she ran to the bathroom and pulled open the door. The kaleidoscope of sickly-sweet scents washed over her – deodorant, bleach, shaving foam, hand cream, make up ...

What was happening to her?

Catherine's stomach lurched and she wretched into the toilet bowl until she was spent.

Afterwards she felt a little better though still very weak and went into the kitchen to find Liam sitting at the table looking worried.

"Are you okay Catherine?"

"Hi, yeah, I guess," she was aware that she was holding her arms around her ribs.

There was an awkward silence between them. Then Liam said, "Do you know that your phone is ringing?"

"Um, oh yes." The truth was she hadn't realised quite what it meant, though she did know it was beeping. "I'll pick up the voicemail."

"What's up?"

"I don't feel well. Been having bad dreams and not sleeping properly for a while."

"Catherine," Liam paused again, "It's more than that, isn't it? I know you and something's wrong." The look on his face was full of concern. "You can talk to me you know?"

It was meant to be a statement but came out as a question revealing his own hurt feelings that she hadn't already confided in him about whatever was bothering her.

"No, no it's fine," she was deeply embarrassed that she had let herself get into such a state. To be honest she had been avoiding Liam lately but mostly because Jojo was hanging around a lot and she couldn't bear another lecture – least of all about how her boyfriend could be a psychopath.

"Catherine, I'm sorry but I have to ask, has Edward hit you?"

"What?" The question shocked her back into focus and her eyes snapped up to meet his. The question was too close for comfort.

"I know, I'm sorry. I'm worried about you."

"Edward would never hit me!"

"No, no of course," Liam looked away embarrassed.

They were close but he must have felt worried to ask such a question. Catherine was not and never would allow a man to hit her and Liam knew it. Any kind of controlling or aggressive behaviour in a man was a deal-breaker for her.

"Why would you think that?"

"It's just, well ... after our conversation about his ex ... Well, you're not your usual bouncy self. And you look like you're in pain, even the way you are standing now. It reminds me of when I was mugged. Now you're not answering the phone ..."

"No, Edward hasn't done anything. I just don't feel well."

Liam paused, "It's not like you," he said.

Catherine felt awful. Liam was her best friend but she couldn't tell him what was going on. It didn't make sense to her, so how could she possibly articulate or explain it to him?

They had a cup of tea together, trying to talk normally, though the conversation was stilted and awkward. It was already evening and she'd slept for almost two days. Her whole body was in pain and trying to hide it from Liam was difficult to say the least, even for a few minutes. She should have been feeling well rested but she didn't. So after the cup of tea she went back to bed.

Her sense of smell had dulled after being sick so she felt calmer. She took some more painkillers and got back into bed, where she lay there feeling strange. When her phone began to beep its crazy frog tune again, she knew it would be Edward. He'd called at least a dozen times and she needed to let him know she was okay.

"Catherine?" came the worried voice.

"Hi," she said, more weakly than she needed.

"Are you okay? I've been going frantic."

"I'm not feeling too good."

"God almighty, you sound dreadful!"

"Sorry."

"Do you want me to come over and give you a little TLC?"

"No, thanks, I want to sleep."

"Are you sure you're okay?"

"Yeah, I'm fine, just a bug or something. Look I'm going to go back to sleep Edward. I'll call you, okay?"

"Oh, okay," he said sounding defeated.

Poor Edward, he'd done nothing wrong but she didn't have the energy to speak to him.

That night she didn't dream one sequential dream, but instead a flow of images passed by her like a conveyer belt.

~ 24 ~
Fight Like A Man

Merwynn lopped alongside Hengist's horse at an easy, steady pace, the wind blowing her shortened hair and her breath coming in pants. The leaf mould soft under her feet.

The morning they had left the monastery Hengist had wanted to kill Adalbert but Merwynn had persuaded him not to. Instead, under Merwynn's instruction, he gave her clothes – leg garments, a loose shirt and leather jerkin, and even a pair of leather shoes. He had to help her put the clothes on as she couldn't raise her arms and the leather jerkin weighed heavily on her painful ribs. Then he had cut her long hair to just above the shoulders and tied it back with a leather thong.

The thought of getting free drove her to endure the pain, and with his help she looked the image of a boy. Then she was loaded into a cart with the food stores to start their journey north.

Hengist had told his men that Merwynn was an orphan boy called Ealdwin who'd been sheltering at the monastery after a Viking attack. That he was taking the boy under his wing. The men just shrugged and accepted his orders without question.

Merwynn spent the first few days going in and out of consciousness, the jarring bumps in the cart causing her such pains that her body knocked her out to alleviate it. Over time, she started to heal and would look out from the cart at the passing countryside. Already she was in unfamiliar territory and further north than she had ever been before.

Several days passed and her injuries healed enough for her to walk beside the wagon, and then one day they came to the biggest river she had ever seen. Stretched from one side to the other was an enormous wooden bridge of arches which reached up and out of the river like some huge monster. Merwynn was terrified but hid her fear under a façade of bravado. None of the others showed any concern and so she girded her loins and walked on without more than the slightest hesitation. She asked the old man driving the cart what the bridge was.

He explained, "Tis a Roman bridge, boy. An' that up ahead," he indicated the market town on the other side of the river, "is Monkchester."

"And the river?"

"Tha' be The Tinanmuðe river, boy," the man said. "Don't yer know nothin'? Best salmon in Northumbria – we'll eat well th' night."

Merwynn shut her mouth and focused on swallowing her fear. The drop from the side of the ancient wooden bridge was shortening her breath and making her feel giddy. She felt a strong desire to look over the edge but kept one hand on the cart to stop her being tempted to do so.

Two days later they paused at the old Roman wall. It was immense and although many sections had either already collapsed or been harvested for the stone, it was the most impressive man-made structure Merwynn had ever seen. The high wall undulated across the countryside as far as the eye could see, following the line of cliffs and curve of the landscape. How such thing had been built she could not even imagine. Worse still, how vicious must the Picts be to warrant building it in the first place. The whole thing unnerved her.

As she got stronger and moved around the camp, some of the other men started to paw at her and a couple had tried to grab her as she passed. Merwynn was not sure if they knew she was a woman or if they didn't care - either way, Hengist took her into his tent telling the men that she was to train as his squire. The men scoffed and made rude suggestions about his wanting Ealdwin's arse all to himself, which irked Hengist, but Merwynn didn't care. At least she was safe from their attentions.

Merwynn was regularly eating meat and drinking ale. Each day, as the fyrd made camp, men went off into the forests and brought back their catch. Sometimes it was red or roe deer, wild boar, goat or sheep. More often it was meagre fare such as squirrels or pigeons. They would rest beside a river and the men would catch ducks, or they would bring back trout and salmon. Sometimes they had nothing at all and would have to make do with bread and ale.

Hengist would always eat at the top table whenever they rested at a castle or monastery, and he saved portions of delicious sweetmeats for her to eat at night. The tastes were so refreshing and she felt nourished and strong. Over the next weeks and months she became fitter and stronger than she had ever been before. She could feel the muscles on her arms and shoulders build.

They travelled through forests and ancient straight Roman roads which, although overgrown were still used, and she had a feeling of wonder at the new places she saw on their travels. This was living. This was freedom.

The company grew as they travelled north gathering more of the fyrd. Some were melancholy, but mostly they were men who laughed and shouted and sang. The constant noise and bustle – so unlike the silence and oppression of the monastery – was uplifting. Merwynn found it fascinating and the freedom with which the men spoke was liberating. They were a rough group and would slap her on the shoulder when they had cracked a joke or punch her playfully on the arm. They would often fight amongst themselves with scuffles breaking out every other day. Merwynn would duck clear and let them get on with it, disappearing into Hengist's shelter until the dust settled. Overall Merwynn liked the men around Hengist. They were fiercely loyal and ready to fight side by side. At night they sat around a fire and Merwynn found the companionship under the stars filled a hole in her chest, as they told stories of heroes and monsters – so much more exciting than the stories of the bible that they told in the monastery.

As they travelled north, they came across a village pillaged by Vikings but there was little they could do. The attackers had come, struck and left again, taking their spoils, slaves, and even their own dead, away with them. All they left behind was burnt out huts, and the mutilated corpses of the people they had massacred. Each tortured face a picture of terror, their last moments stripped bare and their bodies torn apart.

The survivors, if there were any, were nowhere to be seen. If they had returned from their hiding places Merwynn knew that they would flee again on seeing the fyrd appear. To these people any band of men could be as bad as another. And having seen how the fyrd would treat their native residents she could understand. They could strip a village of their food stores and menfolk in the blink of an eye.

Further north they came across people fleeing south from the northern pagan invaders. It seemed like nowhere was safe in the war-ravaged countryside. The fyrd never stopped for long, and never offered any help. They just moved on towards the north, pushing back the small bands of heathens that had roamed into Northumberland.

Merwynn was learning to fight. She had been given a sword and shield by Hengist – a great gift that took her breath away. The sword hilt was leather with silver embossed into it in two coiled bands. The scabbard was equally precious, on a leather belt, and again the same silver pattern hammered into the leather. She loved that sword, wielding it in wide circles to get the feel. She felt that it gave her great power and Hengist seemed delighted with her reaction.

Although she had seen at least a score of winters now, the men thought her only a young man not yet fully grown. They took it upon themselves to train her, saying her orphaned education was sorely lacking. Her muscles strengthened as she wielded her sword in the patterns they taught her. Although she hurt from the exertion, it was a good pain - a healthy happy aching of her body which kept her focused and showed her she was alive.

The men taught her to use a spear as well – in fact that was the first weapon she was to use. The spear, a knife, and the shield were the most used weapons. Her sword was for thrusting and stabbing, or for slicing down on an attacker, not for clanging and chipping on another sword or a shield. Swords were highly valued and parrying other sword blows was a good way of ruining a perfectly good weapon, the sharp edges would be gouged beyond repair. Instead she learned to use a short knife with her shield and spear - her sword hanging at her belt as she fought surrounded by the ealdorman's men in the shield wall.

Then came the battles. There were many of them, mostly small skirmishes to start with, which the ealdorman's men won – but the further north they went the bigger the battles became. Merwynn fought alongside the men, side by side. At first, she was terrified as the blue painted maniacs rushed their shield wall, but she held firm, supported either side by burly strong men who repelled them. She stabbed and slashed alongside the others and plunged her knife deep into human flesh. In the pile of writhing bodies she couldn't see who she'd skewered but the first time it happened she nearly froze on the spot. The shield wall held firm though and the press of men forced her back into action, stabbing, pushing, roaring.

After that first skirmish was over Merwynn felt more alive than she had ever been before. She could not wait for the evening to couple with Hengist and had sought him out, this time pushing him down onto his back and mounting astride him. She was powerful, alive and free and the coupling took them both by surprise.

At harvest time the fyrd were sent home and the court, including Hengist, and his servant Ealdwine, wintered in some grand hall. Sometimes the hall had musicians who played sweet music whilst they ate – songs that made Merwynn want to weep with joy or bang the table with the other men in time to a bawdy taunt. The ones that she loved the most though, were songs of their own adventures and battles that Merwynn herself had fought in. Then spring arrived and they were back on the road again. Merwynn saw many winters and many halls.

Remembering the things she had learnt in the physic garden Merwynn took herbs to ward off any unwanted conceptions - and although she thought a couple of times that she might be with child she did not carry for long. She suspected that too many blows of Adalbert's fists into her soft belly had done more permanent damage. So, mercifully, hiding her sex only involved binding her breasts, cutting her hair and using thick cloths in her breeches during her monthly courses.

At night, Merwynn and Hengist coupled in tents, or in the forest, or in strange rooms by the light of a fire. Caressing, sensual and passionate, sometimes rough, urgent and exciting. Their naked abandonment was a forbidden pleasure. Forbidden by his father as well as Merwynn's church – but for Merwynn it was made all the more enjoyable for defying the God that had deserted her.

Seasons turned, and the war continued. Merwynn was happy living like a boy in a man's moving court and for the first time she felt truly alive.

She was still bonded to Hengist but was happy to be so. She learnt to laugh, long and loud. She was free and she was happy. The northern enemy they fought had a new name – the Kingdom of Alba. Their king, Cináed mac Ailpin, was a ruthless and murderous man who first invaded the northernmost Northumbrian lands of Lothian and then pushed south into Bernicia. Six times he had tried to defeat the Northumbrian army and six times he had failed.

Then one day Merwynn found herself standing at the edge of a wide-open space. Her body lean and muscular, her stance strong and cat-like ready to pounce. Her shield ready and waiting should it be needed. She and the men watched a tent be erected in the middle of a field, as kings and nobles had sat down to talk. Two armies faced each other, nerves jangling and weapons at the ready. An eerie silence hung over them as each strained to hear any treachery first-hand. But talk is all they did.

After years of battles and so many dead, it was resolved with a conversation. Cináed mac Ailpin, and King Osberht of Northumbria divided the region of Lothian giving the Alba Kingdom some much needed farmland. Apparently, the lands north of the river Foirthe were mountainous and hard to till. In return the king of Alba would leave Northumbria unmolested.

The war was finally over.

~ 25 ~
Worlds Collide

By the Saturday morning Catherine was growing a little stronger, and it gave her feeling of optimism. Her stomach was rumbling so she struggled weakly out of bed and made herself something to eat. Being the weekend at least she didn't have to go into work until Monday lunchtime. She still felt drained but hadn't realised quite how ill she'd been until she started to feel better. By the afternoon she was strong enough to shower which helped, but the chemical smells still cloyed at her throat. Feeling clean again she texted Edward to say she was on the mend. She got no reply. In the late afternoon she tried phoning him but it went to voicemail, and texted again asking, *"Is everything okay?"*

Still no response.

"Okay," she said out loud, "be like that."

By the time early evening came around it was starting to eat at her. He had never been this quiet before and it was particularly annoying because he'd said he'd been worried about her. Not now though, obviously.

By the time Monday came around Catherine was feeling stronger, but deep down was confused and hurting. She had still not heard from Edward but had adamantly refused to message him again. She had her next appointment with Bastian first thing and she needed to talk to him about what had been going on but was also nervous that he'd think she'd lost the plot entirely. The detail that she was now dreaming was unbelievable – not to mention the physical manifestation of her dreams causing her to be ill.

As always Bastian took her news in his stride. "So, you went with this army to fight the Scots?"

"Yes," she said, "though I didn't see much fighting, I think I was shielded from it somehow … like a mascot or a child. They trained me but didn't let me into the thick of the fight, almost like they knew I was female." Articulating the idea made Catherine realise what her Saxon alter-ego hadn't, "Maybe the men knew all along?"

"Well, it's not unheard of, even at that time."

"What do you mean?"

"I've been looking into that time-period, Vikings, Saxons and stuff, because of our sessions – and particularly into why a woman might have been dressed as a man. There is a legend of one woman who posed as a priest and even became Pope in the first half of the 9th Century. I think she's referred to as Pope Joan. The story goes that she used the name Pope John VIII, and they discovered she was a woman when she went into labour! The crowd literally tore her, and the baby, apart."

"So not only a woman but an immoral one! At least one other person had to have been in on it," Catherine laughed, though in truth she didn't find it all that funny.

Bastian merely smiled. "After that it was said that the Popes were all crowned sitting on a throne with a hole in the seat so that they could be checked for having testicles." He paused for a moment, then added. "It's unlikely to be true, but it was reported on in the 13th Century which shows that it may have been more common than you think."

"What, cross-dressing or immorality."

"Both!"

At that they both laughed.

"I do know that in the early days of Christianity there weren't so many restrictions. I believe that a rule book of canon law was brought in by the Catholic church as late as the 12th Century to consolidate its ranks and reaffirm the rules on celibacy amongst priests. They wanted to try and curb the immoral behaviour of the masses, and there were reports of bishops running brothels. I think that's when the confessional was started, to ensure that the rules were kept. They used to run monasteries and convents together until the 'immorality' issues became too pronounced and then they were split up."

"How do you know all this?"

"There's not much information around the time, but there is some – bits and pieces. I've been reading up on it – even read the Venerable Bede. It's fascinating stuff. There are over 30 saints who were women dressed as men for a variety of reasons. It may have been the only way a woman could get an education for a start – though usually it was that the woman suffered a personal crisis and then reinvented herself as a man. One saint was a prostitute who converted to Christianity, changed her name and dressed as a man. No-one discovered her real sex until after her death. And St Eugenia who became a monk while disguised as a boy and was so convincing that she became abbot of the monastery. Then after rebuking the sexual advances of a local woman she was brought to court on obviously false charges of fathering the woman's child. She proved her innocence only by baring her breasts in public."

"So do you have an idea when this was all happening to me?"

"I've been thinking about that. The Vikings were raiding on and off throughout the 8th and 9th century but didn't invade

England until the second half of the 9ᵗʰ century. So, I think that it has to be prior to that Danish invasion."

"That sounds about right."

"Then I think another historical fact may be of use. We also know that Kenneth McAlpine invaded Northumberland around 850AD. He's supposedly the man who united the land and raised his own people - the Scots, who were originally from Ireland - over the Picts. The border between the Scots Kingdom and Northumberland used to be the Forth River but McAlpine pushed south from the kingdoms of Fife and Dalriada. He burnt what is now Edinburgh to the ground. There was some campaign at that time to push him back. So maybe that was the war you experienced."

"Maybe. I never knew that Edinburgh used to be part of Northumberland!"

Bastian laughed, "I suppose it's not a part of history they generally teach at school."

Catherine was lost in thought for a moment – a firm date to place what was happening, mid 9ᵗʰ Century, and in an army facing Kenneth McAlpin. It gave what was happening to her a peg to hang on and some perspective.

"Anyway, shall we?" He indicated the chair.

"Yes," she said with slight anxiety.

The door opened and a feeling of despair mixed with a profound sense of anger hit her full in the chest.

~ 26 ~

Rejection

Merwynn stood naked by an open fire in the middle of a warm and comfortable stone-built room. The walls were covered with thick curtains to keep in the warmth, and there were comfortable furnishings around. Not least an enormous bed that her whole family could have slept in – including the cats. If felt like some grand hall.

They had been at war for nearly three years. She was older than she had been before, and her body had curves. She could feel the muscle on her arms and legs, her ribs no longer stuck out and she had almost forgotten what it was like to feel hungry.

All that was about to be lost.

"Why?" she asked. It was discourteous but she didn't care.

He raised an eyebrow but didn't remonstrate with her. "Because we are to go home. The war is over."

She continued to look at him without comment. That was not an answer.

"Because I am to be married and my future wife is a devout woman. Neither she nor my father would allow us to continue."

"Is there nothing to be done?" She tilted her hips to better catch the light, her only weapon was his desire and she knew how to arouse him.

"I regret it Merwynn, but it is necessary. The marriage will strengthen my standing and has been postponed long enough."

"You tire of me?" she pouted.

"No. Never." With that he pulled her back onto the floor where they lay on soft rugs in front of the fireplace and started to caress her in a way she knew so well.

The tears rolled down her cheeks but he was oblivious to them. She was to be sent back to the monastery, and nothing could be done to stop it.

Merwynn still had time. They were travelling back towards Whitby but when they once again passed the Roman wall, she calculated that she had only a few days left before they arrived. They camped that night in the ruins of a Roman fort, the walls still stood but the roof was gone. They sat around a fire on a late summers evening, the men singing songs and telling bawdy jokes before retiring to their makeshift beds.

The next day Hengist had taken her and a few of his men to a thegn's hall in Monkchester. Hengist had a quiet word with the thegn who produced clothes for Merwynn to wear. A pale blue over-dress on top of a linen shift. The lady of the house helped Merwynn with the laces and together they made the dress more fitting. They took away the boy's clothes she had worn, along with her sword and knife.

Whilst Merwynn was allowing herself to be made up as a woman again, she was thinking how to win Hengist over. There had to be a way – maybe transformed into a woman again he would relent and take her home with him. That night their love making was intense and urgent. Merwynn clung to Hengist and he to her and she knew that he could never resist her, never let her go.

The next morning they set off again, this time Merwynn riding beside Hengist on a horse of her own, dressed in fine clothes and her mother's cloak about her shoulders. Although uncomfortable in the women's clothes it was good to feel equal to the man she had loved for so long. She was a high-born lady again and hopeful for the future.

As they approached the Tinanmuðe and the long Roman bridge Merwynn spotted a cart waiting at the side of the road. In it were four monks. She looked sideways at Hengist long and hard but could see no hint of alarm or concern. The monks appeared to be selling honey wine, so Hengist suggested they stop and refresh themselves.

As soon as Merwynn set foot on the ground two of the monks grabbed her by the arms and shoulders and dragged her backwards. She screamed and tried to break free, she instinctively reached for her knife but it wasn't there. Her shortened hair swung loose - her linen head wrap having fallen to the ground as she struggled against her captors.

Merwynn frantically looked to Hengist, sure that he was attacked as well, but saw him calmly atop his horse. Her fear for him turned to confusion - then his betrayal dawned on her - and the confusion exploded into rage.

Merwynn screamed obscenities at him, called him a coward and a cheat, a man without honour or spine. Although those trying to hold her attempted to cover her mouth she bit or spat at them and continued to scream at Hengist.

Hengist stuck out his chin and swallowed hard. With a look of determination, he threw down a leather bag, containing her few possessions. Then he turned and rode away over the wooden bridge, his thegns with him. Not once did he or any of them turn back.

She screamed long after he was out of sight.

Merwynn fought the monks all the way to the cart, then a third monk picked up her legs and they put a bag over her head. They tied her hands behind her and her legs beneath her and threw her in the back. Still she did not stop struggling. She felt a blow to the side of her head. Then nothing.

~ 27 ~
Tynemouth Priory

The tears were still on Catherine's face when she came back into Bastian's company. She cried into her hands for a while and then realised that Bastian was patiently holding out a tissue.

"I'm sorry," she sniffed, taking it.

"What for?" he said genuinely surprised by the apology. "You are working through something you need to go through; maybe this act of dismissal is a route cause of issues in this life."

She thought about that. Had she been afraid of dismissal, of failure? Yes, she had. Her fanatical work ethic and the effort she put into everything she did – was that all because she was afraid of being rejected?

She dried her tears and gave herself an emotional shake.

"Relax for a bit," Bastian said. "I'll be back in a minute." He left the room and she found herself sinking back into the chair, grateful that she didn't have to move straight away.

What was it about rejection that hit home so hard with her? Had it been her mother, being rejected by the one person who was supposed to love her unconditionally? One of her earliest memories was that of trying to climb onto her mother's lap and being pushed away. She can't have been much older than 4. She had started to cry and her grandmother had appeared, given her a sharp smack on the back of her legs, and then led her out of the room. What had possessed her to think her mother would cuddle her she had no idea. The woman was made of stone. She had rarely seen her mother after that. Her grandfather had hardly ever even said a word to her, a grumpy, aloof old man who was disinterested – he had rejected her as well. Her grandmother had hardly been loving either, but she had been the only one who even had the time of day for Catherine. Eve had taught her to read before she had started school, and read she did, anything and everything that she could get her hands on. However, Eve had also told her not to believe the nonsense of the fantasy stories. She could hear her now, *'Remember that the prince never saves the princess in real life, that poor people don't magically find riches, and that only hard work and minding your own business will ever get you anywhere.'*

Catherine thought back to school and the friends that she had. She had never been allowed to go on playdates so it made keeping 'in' with a crowd rather difficult. Eve had always said that Catherine should not *'inflict'* herself on others, and best to concentrate on her studies instead. She was right after all, those so-called friends didn't hang around and Catherine's qualifications had proved to be more useful. In reality, Catherine had rejected her school peers rather than the other way around.

As for boyfriends - Catherine felt a stab of pain at Edward's sudden silence but swallowed it down. In most of her relationships it had been Catherine who had done the rejecting. She would see the writing on the wall when a relationship was coming to an end and usually chose not to drag it out.

So why did this rejection, this Saxon girl being tossed aside by her lover, make her feel so wretched and so hurt? Catherine went over the details again in her mind, trying to remember as she allowed the thoughts to wash over her.

Merwynn had no idea of what time or distance had passed as the cart jolted and bumped along the road. She lay still and tried to get some bearing, tried to hear what the monks were saying to each other, but they were not talking. She had dreamt fitfully of Adalbert and the sour smell of his skin. In waking she promised herself that, if he was still at Whitby, then the very first thing she would do would be to geld him and then cut his throat. She knew it meant her life – she had no money to pay a wergild - but she would never allow a man to treat her like that again.

The cart stopped. A few breaths later, the monks grabbed her bound arms and dragged her out the cart. As she was pulled to her feet, she tried to get her bearings. She could hear the cry and squeal of gulls close by, and taste the salt tang of the sea, so she knew they were at the coast.

"Whitby," she muttered to herself bitterly.

She started to struggle again as the hood was pulled off her head. Then she felt a hard slap across her face. She looked up to see one of those she had known before, one who had survived the Viking raid and come with her to the shared monastery at Streoneshalch.

"Well met my old friend, and welcome to Benebalcrag," she said. The words were kind but her face was hard and disapproving. She nodded once over Merwynn's shoulder and the monks grip relaxed.

Allowed to stand on her own Merwynn turned and glared at the monk, who took a step backwards and then retreated.

The nun reached up and tried to smooth down Merwynn's shortened hair, "My, aren't you looking wild and windswept."

Merwynn shook her head and pulled away, and the nun sighed as she removed her hand. "Very well." She signalled to two very large and heavy nuns who came up to Merwynn and grabbed an arm each. "I can see you need time to readjust."

Merwynn refused to speak and jutted out her chin. She would not give them the satisfaction. She inspected her surroundings as the nun gathered up the leather bag.

Before her was an imposing sight. A cliff-top, wind-swept, stone-built settlement which was nestled on a peninsular of rock surrounded on three sides by steep cliffs. On either side there were beaches far below, on the far side only the wide-open sea. The only route into, or out of, the settlement was through an imposing high stone wall which was topped by a wooden balustrade, in the middle of which stood a fortified twin towered gatehouse. It made Streoneshalch's defences look pathetic.

The burly nuns marched Merwynn through between the towers, and as she mutely allowed herself to be ushered in, she took in her surroundings.

Just inside the walls were the smaller wooden huts and work sheds, where the animals were housed and gardens were tended away from the salty sea breeze. Beyond them were several imposing large stone-built halls. And towering over it all was the church. Merwynn had never seen such a tall imposing building. It looked as if it had stood there forever and the sheer solid grandeur of it took her breath away. This was the same type of stone she had seen at the Roman wall and she wondered whether they had indeed got the building materials from there. The windows were made of stained glass, all colours making up simple pictures that shone with the light of the sky through them.

This was the place that she had been told about, the place which had been built on Pen Bal Crag, the defensive clifftop headland at the Tinanmuðe mouth. It was a priory built to withstand the Viking raids. It had withstood attacks already. This was the resting place of two kings, Oswin King of Deira and Osred II King of Northumbria. This was a pilgrimage site, a sacred place. This was where the nuns of St Hilda had come to remain safe from pagan attack.

Struggling against the firm grip of her arms, Merwynn looked over her shoulder and watched as two monks pushed shut the embossed wooden gates behind them, sealing them inside.

This was Benebalcrag, the monastery, and it was to be her prison.

Not if she could help it.

Catherine awoke with a jump as if she had been given an electric shock, just as Bastian came back into the room. Before Bastian could reach his seat, she was talking excitedly.

"I was at Tynemouth Priory! I didn't recognise it at first as it looks so different to how it does today. They called it another name but it was definitely Tynemouth."

"That makes sense, names and places evolve over time," Bastian replied, intrigued. "What did you see?"

"I saw the cliffs and the walls, but it was when I turned around and saw the gates closing that I recognised it. I watched the last glimpse of the countryside and my freedom disappearing, beyond the moat, in front of the gates." Catherine swallowed hard, "I was being dragged inside. I didn't want to go but had no choice. It was not only that though, there was something else."

"How do you mean?"

"I had an utter dread of being in that life again ... of being unwanted and a burden ... taken somewhere that I know I wasn't welcome ... used and discarded ..." Catherine trailed off.

Bastian leaned forward, "Go on, this is important."

Catherine's eyes flickered with recognition, "I've felt this dread before. It's a pattern, isn't it? The same fear, the same sense of rejection and entrapment, repeating itself?"

Bastian nodded, his gaze intense. "Exactly. These memories, they might be more than just echoes of the past. They could be reflecting patterns in your own lifetime."

Catherine's thoughts raced. "I've always felt unlovable, like I am unworthy ... like I'm reliving through the same rejection over and over again, but in a different setting."

Suddenly the walls seemed to be closing in. She wanted to get out of there but was compelled by good manners not to make a run for it. She could feel something inside her skin shrinking back in terror at the modern world and clawing at the inside of her chest to break free.

"Are you okay?" Bastian asked looking directly into her eyes.

"Yes, yes I'm fine, but I've realised that I'm late for work."

"Before you go," he said, "I want you to think about something."

"Yes?" she looked up from the coat that she'd already reached for.

"You need to think about why are you revisiting this lifetime, why are you remembering what she experienced? In essence, what does she want you to understand?"

Catherine paused, with realisation dawning. "You mean there's a reason I keep returning to these memories? That there's something in my life now echoing that feeling of being rejected and unlovable?"

"Your mind is revisiting this in more detail than I've ever seen before. Usually when there is a specific pattern it means there is a lesson that needs to be learnt or an action needed to be taken. I want you to look at your own life and think. Is there anyone from the past that has come back into your life in the present? Is there a pattern repeating itself?"

Catherine nodded, a newfound clarify in her gaze. The memoires were not just haunting her; they were guiding her to confront her deepest insecurities and fears about love and belonging.

Catherine left Bastian's office with a lot on her mind and started to walk down the bitterly cold street. Someone else who could have been with her in a previous life? Who though?

Her boss, her friends, Edward? But who would he have been back then? Then the image of the violent monk came into her head with a physical jolt to her body.

She felt sick. She tried to eradicate the image, tried to think of something else. Shona's face swam through her mind and her words. *You don't know him!* Had it been him who had put the girl in hospital, was her subconscious trying to warm her about Edward? Catherine didn't want to believe it, didn't even want to consider it, but each time she thought his name she saw the monk's face and her gorge rose as all the images of what the monk had done came flashing back into her mind. She shook her head trying to clear it.

She had another idea. One by one she went through her friends, family and colleagues, in her head. As she made a visual image and mentally said the name another face superimposed itself onto the image. Nuns, monks, soldiers, serfs, thegns came up to the surface of her mind.

Every one of them recognised – people she had met in a past life revisited in this one.

"Liam," she said to herself and there stood the little girl who had been taken from under the haystack by the Viking raid. Catherine teared up at the thought of what had befallen that poor child. Did that explain Liam's alternative attitude to life, his difficulty with long term relationships, his escapism into a gaming world of dungeons and dragons, even his need for dope?

She felt the familiar stab of pain and guilt for letting go of the little girl and leaving her to that fate.

Catherine's phone rang and shattered the feeling as she reached for it. The grey screen showed Edward's number and she had a stab of disgust as the hated image of the monk appeared in her mind. She swallowed hard and answered. "Hi."

"Hi," he replied in a cold and flat voice.

"Where have you been?"

"Had some family stuff to deal with, I'll explain later," he said. "How are you feeling?"

"Better now."

"Good."

"I called you, but you didn't answer."

"Yeah, well. As I said, I've been going through something myself." His usual enthusiasm and spark seemed to have vanished. He was clearly finding this conversation difficult, as was she.

"Right. Well I have to get back to work."

"Can we meet up tonight?" he asked.

"I don't think so," her temper was rising. How did he think he could blow her off like that and then get back into the swing like nothing had happened?

"We need to talk," he said with an air of surprise at her attitude.

"No, I don't think that we do."

"Catherine, you don't understand. It's not ..."

She cut across him. "Look Edward, I have enough on my plate without someone messing me around. I don't need this," she hung up the phone. Catherine was seething inside though logically she couldn't say what he'd done that had made her so angry.

MARY TURNER THOMSON

Every person she passed on her way into work seemed to have shadow, a second person superimposed upon them, following them around.

It was like she was still in a dream, but she knew she was wide awake. Then she caught sight of her reflection in a dark shop window and superimposed inside her frame she could see a different face looking back at her as well as her own. Wild red hair underneath her straight black locks. Green eyes, behind her hazel ones. Passion and fire behind her controlled façade. The other girl looked calm, curious and confused all at the same time. The fleeting image frightened Catherine and she moved on.

Catherine's boss looked peeved as soon as she walked through the door, he got up to talk to her before she had even taken her coat off.

"What happened to you?" he asked.

She glared at him trying to see if he had an alternate entity superimposed inside him but she saw nothing.

"What do you mean?" she felt defensive and off balance.

"Well, apart from the fact that you are late, you look like hell."

"Thanks," she realised with a stab of guilt that she had forgotten to mention the hypnosis appointment. She could feel her usually controlled temper rising again.

"Seriously Catherine, what's going on? You've not been yourself lately and I'm worried about you."

"Right," she was getting positively surly.

"Well?"

"Well what? I'm fine. I was ill. I'm going through some stuff, but I'm fine. I'm always fine."

"I don't think so."

"What are you saying?" Her voice raised more than she had meant it too.

170

"I think you need to take some more time off, sort yourself out."

"Sort myself out?"

"I can't have you in front of our clients like this Catherine, it's not professional."

"Are you firing me?"

"No. Not firing you, I am asking you to take some time out to get yourself back on track."

He was being calm, reasonable and understanding. It grated horribly.

Catherine felt like she was being dismissed again. Discarded and rejected - again. Work had always grounded her and she loved her job, but now it all seemed so irrelevant and cloying. What she did in her employment seemed so petty and pathetic in the grander scheme of things.

"No."

"No? No what?" He looked confused.

She paused then turned on her heel saying, "I quit."

As she walked away, he called after her, "Catherine, there is no need to do that. You're a good employee and I value your contribution. I just don't think you're fit to work at the moment. Catherine …?"

The rest of what he said was drowned out by the distance growing between them.

Catherine marched around the corner and leant against a wall. "What's happening to me?" she gulped back a sob. She had lost her boyfriend and her job in less than an hour. But she refused to be humiliated and discarded again. She wanted to be the one in control, but to do so she was destroying everything that was important to her.

Edward called again but she didn't answer. She had a burning rage inside of her that she didn't want to contain. A fury that was about to explode - heightened because she couldn't pinpoint why.

There was so much noise – everywhere – the roaring of traffic, mindless music blaring, car doors slamming and banging as people got in and out. She tried to take a calming breath, but the pollution choked her. And the people. There were so many people everywhere she looked. A man talked in a loud voice into a phone as he passed. A group of teenagers squealing at something they found amusing on the other side of the road. A couple walking up the street laughing. What did they all have to be so happy about? It was flippant and seemed degrading, even irreverent.

Each passing bus grated, each laughing teenager in a short skirt irked.

"Get out of my head," she groaned.

Catherine flagged a taxi and went home, her head in her hands trying to block out the noise. Liam was out and she lay in her bedroom with the blinds and the door shut. The cold darkness felt good and she started to feel calmer.

She must have dozed off for a while because the next she knew Liam was knocking on her door.

"Telephone," he said.

"Huh?"

Liam came into her room and handed her the house phone. "Telephone." He said again as he thrust the black plastic lump into her hand and walked out.

"Hello," she was still half asleep.

"Catherine, it's me, don't hang up."

"What do you want Edward?"

"I didn't want to tell you like this but ... it's my sister. It's Fiona."

"What about her?" Something in his voice worried her.

"She tried to commit suicide, Catherine."

"What?" She sat up, her blood now pumping hard and her thoughts tumbling together, "How?"

Edward caught his breath in a sob, seemed to ground himself and then started again. "She took pills with a bottle of vodka."

"Edward, no! Is she okay?"

"She's sedated at the moment, in hospital. She's out of the woods ... physically at least, now. I am sorry I didn't answer you at the weekend, it's just ... I know how you feel about suicide Catherine and I couldn't face you."

"Oh Edward, I had no idea. Why? I don't understand."

"I didn't think she was depressed, at least not THAT depressed. She never said anything to me. I hadn't seen much of her the last few months - I've spent most of my time with you."

Catherine was shocked, and then offended. "Are you saying this was because of me?"

"No! No, of course not! That's not what I meant. She's been obsessed with all this past life nonsense. She left me a voice message talking about not wanting to be murdered again and that falling in love would be pointless. It's all because of that bloody hypnotist and over some random dreams she had. She tried to kill herself over nothing – nothing at all."

Catherine knew in her bones that it was not *just nothing* – indeed reality and the past seemed to be clashing together in her own life - and she could see why Fiona might have thought ending her life a way out of the torment. "Edward, I'm sorry about Fiona, but I don't know what you want from me."

"What do I want from you?"

She could hear the hurt in his voice.

"I want to get through this. I want your support."

Catherine opened her mouth but no words came out. She pictured Shona's face in the mirror as she said, 'Clever, *very clever*'.

Edward sniffed, "I don't know why she would do this, it is the very last thing I would expect from her. I don't understand it. Look, Catherine, can we meet up?"

With immediate and intense clarity Catherine knew two things. Firstly, that she didn't want to meet him at the moment – she felt scared of Edward. She was certain that he could not have hurt his sister but Shona's warning was still in the back of her mind – that he was dangerous. Surely not. Secondly, she knew that she had to go back to Tynemouth. She needed to resolve her own issues before she was driven over the edge herself.

"I'm going on a trip, only for a few days, but I'll call you when I get back."

"Oh," he said. Then after a long pause and he added, "Okay."

"I'll call you when I get back," she repeated, "and Edward?"

"Yes?" he said in a very small voice.

"I am so sorry about Fiona."

With that the conversation ended and she said goodbye. She then packed an overnight bag and jumped into the car to drive to Tynemouth. It was already evening but she felt confined and claustrophobic. She had to get out of there.

~ 28 ~

Benebalcrag

Life at Benebalcrag was simple enough and had Merwynn gone there instead of Whitby, after the Viking attack in Hackness, she might have been happy. Now it was a prison.

Merwynn made her first bid for escape the same day she arrived, before the hated bells even peeled for supper. The two nuns who guarded her were fast though and caught her almost immediately. When they took her back to her cell their punishment was swift and hard, the big sticks they carried leaving bruises on her legs that made it hard to walk for the next two days.

In the first few days she tried again but she didn't even make it to the gates. The shout would go up and from everywhere monks and nuns chased her like a pack of wolves after a chicken. Once she had thought she might make it, then a monk stepped out from behind a shed and punched her full in the face. When she woke up, she was back in her cell, her guards waiting for her to wake so they could once again teach her a lesson in humility.

She was shadowed everywhere by the two burly nuns – each still carrying big sticks which they weren't afraid to use. Merwynn wondered how much coin Hengist had parted with to ensure her imprisonment. She bitterly hoped it had cost him dearly.

Days turned into weeks and Merwynn's two guards watched her every waking move. At night she was escorted to her stone-built cell and the door barred from the outside. No escape, but at least there was no Adalbert either.

The small group of nuns of St Hilda that had come from Hackness had moved north to the Benebalcrag priory shortly after Merwynn had left Streoneshalch. The irony of their move which would have saved her from Adalbert without going to war, was not lost on Merwynn. However, it was not the reason they had left. The impressive walls and modern settlement of Benebalcrag was a blessing that they wanted to see for themselves.

After a few weeks Merwynn was set to work. She point-blank refused to enter the smithy or the pottery, even when threated with the cudgel. She did, however, condescend to work in the kitchens and the gardens, tending the herbs and the vegetables, as well as the animals. Being outside provided a sense of freedom compared to the feeling of entrapment indoors, and it gave her the opportunity to scrutinise the walls, searching for any possible means of escape.

Weeks turned into months and still Merwynn was guarded. She became used to the rhythm and flow of the priory. A sophisticated monastery which produced beautiful books – priceless works of art. Merwynn was told that they didn't compare with those being produced at Lindisfarne, but they still made Benebalcrag a wealthy and powerful settlement. Food was plenty and her room was comfortable but Merwynn felt like a caged animal, waiting for the slaughter.

Months turned into seasons. Merwynn learnt to behave like a demure penitent. She laughed and joked with her watchers. She put them at ease offering them sweat treats that she snuck from the kitchens and gossiping about others in the priory. They started to relax with her and although they followed her everywhere, they started treated her like a friend instead of a prisoner. They no longer carried their big sticks.

The seasons changed and changed again. Years passed. Merwynn's hair grew long again and she became part of the community, a devout and regimented member of the priory. To the congregation she was a saved woman, her madness cured - a lost sheep returned to the flock.

Inside, though, Merwynn was more determined than ever. She would be free, however long it took.

~ 29 ~

Cliffside

Catherine drove into the night on almost deserted icy roads, the sky clear and the stars glaring down at her. The journey was driven in silence as her thoughts circled like gulls around her head. The quiet drive felt like a small salve on her jangled nerves.

She arrived in Tynemouth in the early hours of a bitterly cold February pre-morning. She was too preoccupied to get a hotel or to interact with other people so she stayed in the car, parked alongside the Priory that seemed so familiar to her. She thought she might be losing her mind, with no idea what was real and what was not any more. She didn't want the usual comfort of a bed and even hunger seemed to elude her.

She couldn't sleep. All that had happened flashed through her mind over and over. She tried to put it in order but her thoughts tumbled around making it impossible to make sense of anything. The random memory with Jon, Edward, Vikings, imprisonment, Bastion, rejection, Fiona, dancing, betrayal, Shona, suicide ... Tynemouth.

She couldn't fathom why it had all happened and how she had ended up there. Only six months earlier she had been happy, settled, employed and sane. She used to sleep soundly and wake refreshed. Now sleep was unwelcome and often painful. Reality was this, now. This uncertainty, this fear. But fear of what? The universe seemed so big, so unkind, and she seemed so very small.

The birds started singing in the raw morning air. A new day was about to begin and the world would awaken once more.

Catherine's stomach grumbled and with a strong desire for coffee she left the security of her car to go in search for an early morning cafe. She found an open cafe and ordered a cup of ordinary black coffee. The man serving her at the counter gave her a funny look but she didn't care.

"You okay?" he asked.

She looked him straight in the eyes and said with a defensive tone "Yeah, fine. Where's your loo?"

He shrugged and pointed her towards the back of the cafe.

It wasn't the most salubrious bathroom she had ever encountered but it was at least clean. She looked in the cracked mirror. The other girl was still there but this time the reflection didn't frighten her. This time she took a good long hard look.

She was smaller than Catherine, with long wild red hair which hung loose below her shoulders. Her skin, weathered and freckled, held a unique beauty in its distinctive combination. She had a steely look about her though, a hardness born out of survival. Her eyes bored into Catherine with the same scrutiny as well.

Superimposed on her own conscious thoughts she could feel the girl's emotion, understand the redhead's thoughts about what she saw. Catherine could feel the girl's dismay at what she had become, how weak and soft Catherine was. She looked out on her almost like a poorly educated child, someone who didn't know the harsh realities and who had been spoilt, but through no fault of their own. In short, the girl pitied Catherine.

The girl had seen so much, and Catherine – well she had crumbled at the first hurdle. Was this who she was? Was that feeble, sleep deprived, stressed out, woman that she had become, really her?

Catherine looked at herself harder, tried to see the real her and she was shocked by her own reflection, stunned to see how tired, pale and thin she looked. Her hair was lank and her face seemed alien. When was the last time she had smiled?

She pulled herself away from the double reflection and washed her face in cold water. Then she pulled out a comb and tried to tidy her tangled hair. She felt a little better. Then she went back to the much-needed coffee and put the money on the counter. The man handed her two rounds of toast, "On the house," he said.

She wondered how bad she must look to warrant charity, but dismissed it with a mumbled, "Thanks" as she took the plate and the mug of coffee.

She sat down at a plastic table facing away from the man and out of the window. Hunkering down she held the coffee between her hands feeling the warmth enter into her bloodstream. It was comforting and she absently took a bite of toast as well. It helped a lot, and she ate the rest of the toast whilst she thought about what to do.

Tynemouth Priory didn't open for a few hours so she had time to kill. She could wait there, in the warmth. As the sun rose, brightening the world, a bone-chilling wind persisted. Despite the cold, she considered going for a walk in a little while.

"Ah haven't seen you here before, Pet." Came the man's voice beside her. She jumped as she turned to see him wiping a perfectly clean table next to her.

"No, I haven't been here before."

"You new to the area?"

"Just passing through."

"Do you need any help? Looks like you've had a rough time."

It was difficult to read his expression, he seemed to be meaning it kindly, but she caught an edge to his voice which warned her of danger.

Catherine sensed the girl within her recoil from him, stirring a deep sense of nervousness. The emptiness of the café dawned on her, heightening her awareness of her vulnerability.

"No, I'm fine, just slept in the car last night." Why did she tell him that? "I arrived too late to go to my friends. They are expecting me first thing this morning," she lied smoothly. "I had better get going."

With that she drained the last of her coffee and left.

The icy wind hit her as she closed the café door. She wanted away from that bloke although he'd done nothing but seem friendly. The Priory still wasn't open yet as it was long before most rational people were abroad.

Instead she went down onto the beach to the north of the Priory – the one now called King Edwards Bay. A long set of steep steps lead down onto the beach and she absently noted how hard it would be to get up from the bay below without the help of those stairs being there. It would be like scrambling up a thorny cliff. She could see how the peninsular had been viewed as such a defensive position.

She wandered out across the pale sands towards the sea's edge feeling unrestrained but also sandy eyed and exhausted; the waves looked inviting though she knew it would be freezing cold. The girl inside her seemed to relax a little on familiar ground, though she also seemed restless, and that something was trying to pull her in one direction or another.

Catherine didn't know how long she stood there her mind empty and drifting with the tide, but a shiver brought her back to the moment. She turned to look up at the Priory and froze in shock as she looked at the window standing black in the cliffside. The familiar shape and dimensions seemed to wipe away her sleepiness as she felt a full-on rush of adrenaline. She knew that with absolutely clarity it was the same window she had seen in her first hypnosis session. She was rooted to the spot her mind racing, her blood pumping and her spirit soaring into the oblong void of darkness in the cliff.

The window was more than half-way up the cliffside and it looked like it belonged to some sort of ruined tower.

She was holding her breath.

Beyond the sill was darkness and that meant a room was behind it – the room she had been in when she first experienced the Saxon girl dressed as a man?

Catherine had to see the room close up.

As if a starter gun had been fired, she leapt forward at a run towards the cliff, then without pausing at the bottom she started to climb.

Catherine had rock-climbed before and so knew she could do it, but the closer she got the more unstable and steeper the rock became. The tangled nettles and weeds of the steep slope gave way to rocky walls and dangerous footholds but still she pushed forward. She had to see inside that window. She reached a shelf below the opening and could reach out and touch the stone lintel, but she couldn't see in. It was maddening. Calming herself she descended the cliff a little and tried a different riskier route.

Slipping slightly she managed to pull herself up onto the edge of the window sill and could peer over the side into the room.

It was exactly as she had seen it. The cell was a small room and it had a stone bench along one side. The straw mattress on the bed and the wooden cupboard was gone, as was the door, but the doorway was as it had been.

It existed. Not only in her hypnosis session but here, now.

She let herself down from the window ledge and found a safe spot on the cliffside to rest. Turning her back to it she looked at the same view the Saxon girl had seen from inside the room.

It was beautiful and for a moment she felt part of nature.

~ 30 ~

Gwenhild

Life was peaceful and safe at Benebalcrag, but Merwynn still felt trapped. She had to play the part of a penitent nun, a vanquished spirit, cowed and now returned to God. She spoke quietly and only when spoken to. On the outside it looked like she endured her internment with a good grace, but all the while she still planned to escape.

To most, Benebalcrag was a decent place, the monks were straightforward pious men who were proud of their saints and the kings whose remains they protected and revered. The monastery was rich place with donations - from poor men who wished boons from the saints, to the rich who paid for prayers to speed their passing to God's side. It was comfortable and secure with its high walls and strong gates. The nuns of St Hilda who had come there for protection were hard working women who tended the sick and taught the noble children and novices in their charge.

Even though they had imprisoned her, Merwynn held no ill-will for them – the monks and nuns were only doing what they thought was right. So she showed ladylike good manners to all that acknowledged her – and many still did not. Her outrageous behaviour in running off to war dressed as a man incensed some who would never forgive her - not for deserting the church but for betraying her sex. She had even overheard some of the nuns talking about her, saying, "Where would the world be if all women dressed like men and expected to be treated the same. It would be a disaster."

Under her breath Merwynn muttered, "Where indeed!"

She wanted to scream, and run and fight, but she buried it all deep and showed nothing but calm on her exterior. She worked in the gardens and in the kitchens, and although not a slave by name, she felt like it in every other way. When the monastery built a hospital, she began to visit often, bringing herbs and plants from the physic garden. Over time she started to work there as well, ministering to the sick.

Sometimes she would listen to the birds chirping as they called back and forth. She would watch them launch from the trees and fly free over the walls and she would sigh. Had she come to Benebalcrag from her father's house she would have been happy there. Not now though. Not now.

By her second year at Benebalcrag, Merwynn's guards became less burly and more friendly, the priory became busy and her minders were reduced to one at a time. As their attention relaxed, Merwynn started to plan her escape.

She had to get clean away, go as far south as possible - like her mother had when escaping the Picts in her youth. Merwynn planned to travel through Mercia and onto Wessex or Kent. Maybe even travel to foreign lands. Somewhere that no-one knew her. Where she could live free and on her own terms. She had heard that warmer weather beckoned further south and that the Vikings raided less. She imagined going from town to town, finding work with traders or story tellers. She could read, and she had skills. She could even be a mercenary if she was able to get her hands on a sword and shield. None of that would be possible as a woman though, she would need to become a man again.

When traders from Mercia visited Benebalcrag, Merwynn heard them talking about their travels over the lands of the Angles and she desperately wanted to travel with them.

The hospital gave her access to steal items of clothing – always one item at a time, and always the most worn or least cared for. Sometimes items that were torn or bloody that she could explain away as having been discarded. Over time, as new patients passed through the priory, Merwynn would pocket small things that would not be missed. Things that could help disguise her when she made good her escape. A small bag, a belt, a pair of dice, anything that might assist. Although she was frightened of being caught, the stealing at least gave her a rush of feeling something. A silent rebellion against her imprisonment, and a hope for the future.

It was in the hospital that she heard of a cave entrance in the cliffs on the North side of Benebalcrag, which led through a tunnel of caverns right under the river Tinanmuðe. The tunnels led all the way along to Gyruum, where the venerable Bede had once resided. She was not keen on the caves but they could provide a chance of escape. She was watched too closely and couldn't get to the beach but she had discovered another potential entrance within the cavernous cool storerooms, dug deep into the rock within the monastery. Folklore had it that the ancient cave stores connected to the ones on the beach. The day that she had tried to squeeze through the tunnel behind the shelves though, she had found her way barred by rock falls. Sick with disappointment she had to turn around and go back to her imprisonment. At least her attempt had not been discovered.

Then a new nun, by the name Gwenhild, was allocated the task of watching Merwynn. She was a young woman, smaller and plumper than her prisoner, and only a few years older than Merwynn had been when she had arrived at Streoneshalch. The girl jumped at noises and would step closer to her charge as if for protection – she reminded Merwynn of a scared little mouse. The girl's big blue eyes followed her taller charge wherever she went - not with suspicion, but instead with a sense of awe. Merwynn was not sure if she was to be watched by, or to watch over, Gwenhild. She wondered what had happened to the girl to make her so nervous. One thing was clear though, Gwenhild saw Benebalcrag as a safe haven and never wanted to set foot outside the priory complex ever again.

Merwynn tried to befriend Gwenhild with feigned interest in the girl. She could, after all, be turned into an ally in helping her escape. However, as Gwenhild relaxed and started to come out of her shell, Merwynn found that she didn't have to pretend at all. The young girl's re-emerging kind and gentle nature reminded Merwynn of herself when she was younger. Although jumpy Gwenhild still held a joy of living and Merwynn took pleasure in making her smile.

In the mornings, when her door was unbarred, Merwynn felt a growing joy to see it was Gwenhild's face that greeted her. She looked forward to when they talked whilst they tended the gardens, or fed the chickens, ducks and geese. Merwynn told stories of her life which held Gwenhild spellbound. She began to teach Gwenhild tricks on managing the gardens and how to harvest herbs without damaging the plants. Merwynn would laugh when the girl's smooth forehead creased into a frown, each time she didn't understand something that the older woman found quite simple. She started to notice tiny things her guard would do and she was surprised to find them enchanting. The way that Gwenhild wrinkled her nose at smells when learning to identify the different medicinal herbs; her boundless enthusiastic curiosity and desire to learn; the rose tint in her cheeks when she was out of breath. Merwynn was becoming fascinated by her.

When Gwenhild would drift into rumination and was looking lost in sad thoughts, Merwynn would play pranks on her - throwing a bit of earth or water to snap her out of it. The sweet nun's smile was like the morning star that guided Merwynn home. Her light laugh was like gold dust which made Merwynn feel rich in life. Merwynn realised she didn't see Gwenhild as a guard any longer and found herself being more and more drawn to her new found friend.

One day Merwynn was handing Gwenhild a sprig of rosemary to smell when their hands touched and, for a moment, they remained connected. Merwynn looked up to find Gwenhild gazing back at her, eyes wide and intense. Then they both pulled away.

After that Merwynn would find reasons to touch the girl, a hand on her shoulder, a tickle when they were laughing, a hug when she was frightened. Each time Merwynn did not understand the feelings that were welling up inside of her.

Then it happened. Gwenhild's lips found hers, and Merwynn, enveloped in a wave of unexpected tenderness, responded in kind. This kiss was a world apart from those she had known with Hengist. Where his were marked by urgency and demand, Gwenhild's were a whisper of affection, a gentle exploration. The softness of her lips, free from the rough stubble of a man's chin, was like a soothing balm. Merwynn tasted the remnants of sweet berries on her breath, each note playing a sensual song on her senses. The encounter was tentative, yes, but filled with a mutual curiosity and a silent understanding that this was new terrain for both of them.

After that initial, exploratory kiss, a space grew between them, filled with unspoken questions and a tender awkwardness. They continued their day, each moment tinged with the memory of that gentle intimacy.

As night fell and Gwenhild moved to close and bar the door from the outside, Merwynn, driven by a longing that ran deeper than loneliness, reached out. Her fingers traced a tentative path along Gwenhild's arm, their eyes meeting in a silent conversation of desire and understanding. Gwenhild's response was wordless but clear; she closed the door from the inside, sealing them away from the world.

In the soft glow of the night, they discovered each other. Their touches were exploratory and reverent, each caress a word in a language they were only beginning to speak. They kissed with a tenderness that spoke of deep affection and mutual respect, their movements unhurried and instinctual. Their bodies entwined, with no goal, and no agenda - just the unfolding of a shared journey. They learned the contours of each other's bodies, not as physical forms, but as extensions of their spirits. The air around them seemed to pulse with a newfound understanding, a connection that transcended the physical realm.

As they lay in each other's embrace, their breaths synchronising, a profound sense of solace enveloped Merwynn. In Gwenhild's arms, the void of loneliness that had long shadowed her heart began to lift. The intimacy they shared was not just a meeting of bodies, but a silent pact of trust and mutual support.

As sleep claimed them, nestled in each other's arms, Merwynn realised that for the first time in what felt like an eternity, she was not alone. She was understood, valued, and most importantly, loved for who she truly was.

During the day Merwynn and Gwenhild would companionably work side by side rarely touching and not showing any affection for each other. But, when the chance arose, at night they would cuddle up together and talk. Merwynn told her lover all about her life, about her childhood, and her mother. About the Viking raid, and little girl, Cwen, in the haystack. About Brother Adalbert, and Hengist. She shared every detail

of her life wanting Gwenhild to know everything about her. She showed Gwenhild her precious stone snake that she took with her everywhere, and even the silver ring, though she did not tell Gwenhild where she had got it. Gwenhild admired the ring and so Merwynn gave it to her – even though it was the only thing of value she owned.

Then, one day, Gwenhild opened up to Merwynn like a flower. Bit by bit, when they lay naked in bed together, Gwenhild told her lover her story.

Gwenhild's home had been destroyed by a local feud. It had started between two neighbouring thegns - men that had once been friends. A fight ensued and one had killed the other thegn's son. After the second thegn retaliated for that the first thegn laid waste to their whole village. They had been taken by surprise thinking they were too far inland to be in danger from the Vikings. The thegn's men had killed everyone – no matter that they had once been friends. Gwenhild, a freeman's daughter, had hidden herself under a sleeping pallet and as the noise of the killing subsided, she thought that she had survived. Then a hand grabbed her and pulled her out.

Merwynn traced the rough edges of the jagged scar that puckered across the middle of her chest, as Gwenhild shared her story.

"Afterwards … after the bastard had finished …he stood over me and spat in my face. I couldn't move, couldn't hardly breathe. It was like I wasn't in my own body, like I was watching it from afar. Then he drew out his sword and put the point against my bared chest. I thought he was going to order me to get up, to take me away, but then … he just leaned on his sword. He was leering as it cut into me. I think he wanted me to scream, but I didn't. I remember thinking 'better to die'. I don't think I even felt the pain until later." Gwenhild paused for a long time, then started up again. "Then he grunted, kicked me and left. I was still frozen there, my skirts up around my waist and staring at the wall. Staring at the blood of my mother sprayed across it. It was like ... I was dead. Like I had watched it all from eyes that weren't mine. I didn't even move when he kicked me. I stayed like that long after the silence came. I stayed like that until the birds started to sing again – waiting for death to carry me off. Each time I breathed in, I thought would be my last. Then came the pain and I don't remember anything else. They had left me for dead, but not before putting a baby in my belly."

Merwynn felt Gwenhild shiver, and she kissed her head softly.

Gwenhild went on to tell Merwynn that only two others had survived the raid, the young son of the local ealdorman, and his friend from the village. They had been in the forest when they saw the thegn's men creeping towards the settlement. The lads had buried themselves in the soft loam of woods to avoid detection.

Once the coast was clear, the boys had found Gwenhild unconscious, and tended her wounds with fire. They had thought that Gwenhild would die but when she awoke, her desire to save the boys drove her onwards. Together they stumbled across the countryside to the monastery, who took them in to their hospital. She believed that God had saved her. A message was sent to the boy's father – who was so relieved to find his son alive that he paid Gwenhild's dowry to the monastery at Benebalcrag and adopted the other boy into his household as his son's servant. And so Gwenhild had become a nun. Something that never would have been possible to an ordinary village girl.

"At least I am safe now," she said kissing Merwynn's fingers, and cuddling in close, "here with you."

"Yes. Safe. I suppose." Merwynn had an uneasy feeling that Gwenhild was using her - the same way that she had used Hengist. As a protector and a safe haven. She had never loved

Hengist, but she knew him and could control him. Was that all she was to Gwenhild? She wanted to ask Gwenhild to leave Benebalcrag with her, for them to travel together. "Would you ever think about leaving, travelling to other places and seeing a bit of the world."

"No, never!" Gwenhild replied with a shiver. "Why would I ever leave? Go back out there? There's nothing there - nothing but evil and pain. We have everything we could ever want right here."

Merwynn sighed. She didn't have everything she ever wanted. She had peace and quiet, food and shelter, but she didn't have any choice in her life. She didn't have the freedom to live. She knew that one day she would have to decide between freedom or love, and she already knew that no matter how much she loved Gwenhild she could not remain trapped like a caged animal. Even if she did remain at Benebalcrag, it was only a matter of time. Merwynn knew that their relationship would eventually be discovered and Gwenhild would be taken from her. Then she would be back to being watched by brutes. This dream of love was only temporary.

"What happened to the babe?" Merwynn asked.

"I carried it to term. As soon as it was born it was taken away."

Merwynn looked at Gwenhild blankly, expecting more.

"It was the spawn of the devil," Gwenhild replied with uncharacteristic bitterness. "I hope they took it to the cliff edge and threw it off."

"Did you never ask what happened to it?"

"No," Gwenhild turned away from her. "Never."

Merwynn sighed, she would have loved to have been a mother, cradling a babe in her arms and teaching a daughter love – like her mother had with her. At the same time Merwynn had been terrified of it, having seen her mother die in childbirth. Like a lot of things though, Adalbert had taken the choice away from her and it was that lack of freedom to choose that rankled her the most.

~ 31 ~

Awakening

A sense of peace enveloped Catherine as she clung to that cliffside, a fleeting moment of calm. Life was okay, even good for a moment and as she looked out to the sea, she had that familiar pull to jump into oblivion. She had always felt that pull of vertigo whenever she was near a sheer drop. It wasn't a wish for self-destruction or a conscious choice, but a primal instinct she always fought near precipices — a call of vertigo tempting her to surrender to nature's embrace. How easy it would be to let go now, to give up on life itself and just become part of nature. To disappear and avoid all this pain and anguish.

The certainty and finality of death was so attractive that it seemed to pull her outwards. Her desire to jump so strong that she almost let go, but at the last moment she scrambled backwards.

"What in God's name are you doing Catherine?" she said out loud, now shaking with shock. This wasn't right, this was giving up and she was NOT someone who gave up.

Her sudden twist and jerk to regain balance shifted the loose stones below her feet and they started to slip away. She jumped from one foot to the other to regain a hold. Her fingers grasped an outcrop but her toes slipped in her unsuitable shoes. She was left dangling from only one arm, scrabbling with the other arm and both feet to regain a foothold. She tried in vain to get a better hold with the other hand, but she was tiring fast.

Now she was frightened and her heart hammered in her ears. At the same time everything came into focus. She didn't want to die. She wanted to live.

In another adrenalin rush of clear thinking she viewed the descent. She was going to fall. She knew she had no choice in that, but she could influence which way would provide the least dangerous route.

She pushed with her free hand and swung with the last of her strength, launching herself towards the overgrown area full of weeds and nettles. A rough descent but where the stones of the cliffside were dulled. She banged and bumped down, feet first. The thistles slowed her speed, as she tried to keep upright

.

About half-way down she started to tumble and lost the little control she had over the fall. She went head over heels and thought, before she blacked out, that it was all over.

~ 32 ~
The Hoard

Finally, the time had come. They had started to trust Merwynn, started to relax their vigilance on her whereabouts and she was going to be able to reclaim her freedom. Not even the comfortable companionship of Gwenhild made her want to stay.

She had lain beside Gwenhild, softly stroking the sleeping girl's hair. Trying to memorise the curve of her cheek and eyelash, the touch of her warm skin. The sound of her breathing. Even if she was caught Merwynn knew she would likely never see Gwenhild again and knew this was the last time they would touch. She wanted to hold onto that moment, to box it up in her mind and keep it safe. Everywhere she went she would take that memory of love with her.

With a sigh, she crept out of the bed leaving Gwenhild sound asleep. She regretted leaving and knew Gwenhild would be in trouble for not barring Merwynn's door that night, but it could not be helped. As she watched her lover, Merwynn hoped that she would understand – she of all people knew Merwynn best and knew how trapped she had felt. With her heart aching, Merwynn put on her mother's cloak and fastened it around her neck, then she'd put her hand in her pocket. For a moment she hesitated then pulled out the small stone snake that she had carried around for so many years. The talisman that had kept her safe from the Vikings at Hackness, and from the marauding northerners throughout the war. She squeezed it hard within her fist willing it to give her luck, fusing it with all the love that she could. Then she kissed it and laid the gift beside Gwenhild's lovely brown hair. The girl would find it when she woke and Merwynn hoped that she would understand the love in that message. A small salve for the betrayal she would have to endure.

As Merwynn softly closed the door she breathed deeply and then set off. She tiptoed down the corridor and past the sleeping cells, out into the warm night. The salt air was clear and fresh on her face as freedom beckoned, and as she wiped the tears away, she felt hope beginning to build. She pushed thoughts of Gwenhild out of her mind – it didn't help to dwell on the loss. Her heart quickened and her eyes became sharp and focused.

As she had retrieved the bag of clothes and dried food from its hiding place in the gardens beside the wall, she had a little of the excitement she used to feel before going into battle. Then Merwynn had slipped past the monks at the gatehouse, too intent upon their game of dice as usual to notice. Merwynn was pleased to see that, as expected, the monks had not barred the gateway with the heavy wooden cross beam. As usual the beam was leaning against the wall ready should any danger present itself. Instead, it was locked with the metal bolt which slid across from one side of the gates to the other. She started to pull the smooth metal bar carefully across. At first it didn't move and Merwynn had a moment of panic that she might fail. Then she pushed her shoulder to it and the metal moved with a soft scraping sound. It seemed like a scream to Merwynn. She stopped momentarily - every nerve jangling - to see if it had alerted the monks to her escape. No alarm sounded, nor could she see men running to seize her.

The bolt moved easier after that, and Merwynn opened the gate a crack, slipping through as quietly as she could. She pulled the unbolted gate closed behind her, then made her way to the deserted tower at the north side of the cliffs, just outside the priory walls. It was not safe to travel dressed as a woman and the tower that was used for visiting dignitaries, and those not of the Christian faith, would enable her to change with privacy before heading down to the beach.

As she entered the deserted sleeping chamber, she pulled the heavy curtain back from the window and opened the shutters. She had no candle with her to light the room but the summer moonlight was enough to see by. She looked out at the pale silver sands which had been turned black by the night, and the deep blue of the wave peaks highlighted silver by the moon, whilst the white foam kissed the shore with its relentless swell. It was a good night to travel, calm, warm and clear. Should she find the caves inaccessible she could head East on foot until she found some other means of transport across the river.

Smiling to herself, she turned from the window and shook open the bag to empty the items of men's clothing she had gathered together. Linen shirt, leg garments, tunic, belt. Each item reminded her of the people she had tended in the hospital, many whom had died. She was grateful to them all. As she finished dressing, the excitement built further inside her, a new beginning and freedom beckoned. It would be morning before they started to search for her and by then it would be too late. She would be long gone and onto a new life. She wanted to laugh out loud with the anticipation of it.

Then she froze, hearing the small sound below the window. The sharp but distant noise of metal on metal. It sent shivers down her spine. She stepped cautiously forward to the window and looked outside into the night.

That was when she saw it.

The glint of metal on the sea. Then another warning gleam, and another. The reflection of helmets and swords in the moonlight. And not only on the water.

Vikings.

Unlike the numbers that came from one or two dragon headed ships - when twenty or more would descend upon poor unprotected villagers – here were a hoard. Like a swarm of bees, too many to count.

Hell had opened up bringing its daemons with it – a score or more of ships like a black cloud on a dark ocean had appeared around the headland from nowhere. And hundreds of Vikings were already flooding up the sands.

Even Benebalcrag's high walls could not withstand such numbers.

Merwynn backed away, step by step. She had no idea how many had already climbed the cliff, but maybe she had seen them in time. Someone would raise the alarm - but all she could hear was silence. The bells were not ringing. Then she remembered the distracted monks that she had so easily slipped past and worse still, the gate that she had left unbolted and unbarred.

She took another step backwards as she continued to fasten her cloak at the shoulders. Now was the time to run, hide, and get away.

Her back hit the wall and the impact with the stone made her jump into action. Heart pounding she turned and hauled the door open. She ran along the short corridor and up the stone steps. At the top she opened the solid wooden door – just a crack at first - onto the outside wall. She couldn't see or hear any movement in front of the priory – she still had time to escape if she ran now. In the silence she knew that the invaders had not yet been spotted, and in the battle, she could get clean away. Freedom, a new life. A new start.

She stopped. For once it was the absence of the ringing bells that shook Merwynn to her core. She couldn't live with herself if she left her former prison guards to this fate.

She had only ever felt alive when she had faced her daemons and running at the expense of all those souls was a price she was not willing to pay. Not after Cwen. In a moment Merwynn turned back towards the priory. She herself would rouse the monks and bar the gates if she had to.

In the split second that she changed direction she saw them. The Danes were surging all along the incline of the dry moat, up to the gatehouse door.

The night was so quiet, the Viking devils were moving at a crouch as they climbed the incline. Their chain and leather armour muffled by animal skins and oil. They were everywhere and their grimacing faces were masks of concentration.

Merwynn resisted the scream that had clawed up from her stomach. She clamped her jaw shut covering it with her hand, for fear that her mouth would betray her. She only had moments to close the gates before the charge. She slipped back against the wall, her mother's dark cloak hiding her in the darkness and pulled the hood down to cover her face. Ducking inside the gate she saw it was already too late.

Two burly Danes stood over the body of an unrecognisable monk just a few feet inside the gates, his face smashed and bloody. A few paces beyond was another dead man, his throat ripped out. The Vikings were looking into the settlement and didn't see Merwynn as she slipped past them and over the low wall into the physic gardens. Beyond that she slipped through into the paths between the work sheds.

Maybe she could hide and sneak back out once the hoard had passed inside. She knew it was a forlorn hope. Then she remembered the cave in the storage room. They might not provide escape but if she could get to Gwenhild they could maybe hide there until the hoard had left. Merwynn had survived before and maybe they could again.

She made her way around the back of the buildings. It was still dark - the brethren had finished their prayers and already returned to their cells. She wanted to warn someone, to raise the alarm, but what could they do now their precious walls were breached.

She stood with her back to the smithy, even now finding the smell sickening, and cautiously glanced around the corner. The Vikings had reached the gates and swarmed over its threshold unrepelled.

Then the roar went up. Every daemon opened his mouth and cheered with malignant delight as they fanned out and broke into a murderous run. Axes raised and swords flashing. The answering screams came only moments later as nuns were pulled out of their cells and hacked to death. Only when their battle lust cooled would there be a chance of survival, to be violated and taken as a slave – maybe to prolong life for an agonising season or two.

From all directions the monks ran back to the church they had so recently vacated, looking for sanctuary. Merwynn ran as well, making her way round the backs of cells and halls, trying to find a way back out of the killing ground, if she could get to Gwenhild and then to the caves they could at least hide.

Every turn she made drove her further into the centre, as she was shepherded towards the church.

Once there, she would be trapped. She tried to double back only to encounter more Vikings around another corner. She roared in frustration as she skidded to a halt falling backwards in her desperate attempt to change direction and was spotted by a brutal blood covered giant of a Dane. He immediately took up the chase.

She scrambled to her feet and ran as he chased her down between two halls, but her lighter frame saved her in the dark.

She climbed up over the low roof of the pottery kiln and jumped down the other side.

The Viking was too heavy to follow her and took himself off in another direction.

She could not rest though. As soon as she touched the ground again, she was on the run. She couldn't even hide. The Vikings were burning every building and even ensuring the thatched roofs were caved in before leaving any occupants choking and screaming as they died.

The church was at her back. She turned and ran to the door.

"Get out of here!" she cried to the brethren who had accumulated there on their knees, whilst at the same time she scanned the faces for Gwenhild. Most of the monks were weeping and tearing at their own tonsured hair – a few nuns had made it to the church but those that she saw were more composed than the men. Some sat in prayer gazing up at the ornate silver cross which would soon be torn apart as divided spoils.

No-one moved from the church. Not one monk or nun made to leave their beloved sanctuary; the saints they revered, the two stone coffins of the Northumbrian Kings, Oswin and Osred, both betrayed and murdered by their enemies too. They were frantically praying to God for their deliverance. Merwynn knew that God could not stop these daemons. Each pale face showed they knew what approached only moments away; they knew they would join their kings in violent and bloody death.

She yelled in frustration, if only they tried to fight then some might find a way out, a few could escape. She turned her back on the nearly dead believers to face the oncoming enemy alone.

Outside the church, she saw Gwenhild running from the gardens. The look of terror on her face tore Merwynn's heart in two. She had seen that look before, on Cwen's face. Merwynn reached out her arms even though Gwenhild was still twenty paces away from her.

"Run!" Merwynn screamed. But it was too late.

The tall slender Viking chasing the younger woman, caught her by the back of her clothes and drove a sword through her back. The point came through the front of her dress and blood spouted from her mouth as she stopped mid-scream. All the while her eyes locked on Merwynn's. She fell heavily to her knees, held out her hand to Merwynn and then forward onto her face. Gwenhild was dead before she hit the ground. For a moment everything stopped for Merwynn. Stunned and detached she watched as the coiled stone snake rolled out of Gwenhild's hand and came to rest in the tall grass.

Merwynn looked at her dead body and then up at the Viking who had killed her. If only she had a weapon, a sword, or even a knife. She would have at least died killing that one. He bent down and slipped the silver ring off Gwenhild's finger and put it on the end of one of his. A grin on his face like a child with a toy.

The Vikings started to encircle the small church – casually barring the doors and setting fire to the building that would become the monks' tomb. The heat of the rapidly expanding flames blew Merwynn backwards, as the occupants screams became a chorus, like a last hymn. Choking on the thick smoke, Merwynn took the only opening left. She ran towards the cliff top ahead of the tightening band of murderers. She was not free or clear though.

The tall slender daemon that had skewered Gwenhild followed at a slow lope. He was in no rush as she had nowhere to go.

She was cornered.

She stopped at the cliff edge overlooking the now dawn lit ocean. The rocks far below were jagged and lethal. The water exploded onto the cliff beneath her with each breaking wave. The violence of nature seemed appropriate, and it soothed her. It reminded her of the time she had taken the two little girls home to the coast and had seen the ocean for the first time. The awe she felt at its enormity and power. The peace that the ocean gave her that no matter what she went through it would always be there. Everything seemed crystal clear.

Merwynn swallowed the stab of guilt that she always carried with her. This was all her fault. Gwenhild had died and all these monks and nuns were doomed because she had wanted her freedom and left the gates accessible. At the same time she knew, that even if the gates had been barred, this hoard would have broken them down. Her actions had only shortened their suffering. It was fitting though that she should not survive either.

Calmer than ever before, and more in control, she knew what she would do. She knew what mattered to her and what she was prepared to die for.

She turned to face the Viking with her back to the cliff edge.

To her surprise, close up she could see he was a young man maybe only 15 winters, with fine facial hair and not fully filled out. He was still bigger and stronger than her and the menace in his bloodied face was clear.

She stared at him taking in every detail; noting how he held his sword like one well used to wielding it; how one eye was bruised and almost swollen shut from some previous battle; how his long yellow hair was braided; and how his gangly legs flexed as he balanced his weight.

In her calm detachment she could see him falter. Her lack of fear or defensive action seemed to confuse and unnerve him.

A vision of this young man's future flashed into her mind, of being a father holding a new baby boy, a look of pride on his young face. Suddenly she didn't see a demon before her, but just a man.

She noticed that his eyes as he stood poised to strike – they were a vivid blue. Then she saw his eyes widen. She realised that he'd thought her a man but then had recognised a woman's expression that didn't match the garb of a freeman which she wore. It made him pause.

She smiled a genuine, warm smile. That act of uncertainty, that moment of indecision on this young man's part gave her an option. Submit and she might be taken as a slave.

Knowing that, she opened her cloak which she had held around her body and stretched out her arms in the sign for supplication. The cloak stretched out on either side of her like the wings of a bird.

She showed her lack of weapon and stood for a moment as Christ on the cross.

She had a choice and she made a choice. She would not be a slave any more. Not to brother Adalbert, nor to an ealdorman, nor to a church, nor to a Viking. She would choose to be with those she loved instead, her mother, Cwen, and Gwenhild.

She let her body tilt backwards and the last thing she saw was the confusion on the Viking's face as she fell away from him.

She felt the fall and she didn't scream, the air rushing past her, the salt smell of the sea lasting longer than she expected - all her senses relishing her last heart beats of life. She experienced a moment of weightless peace as all the noise, smoke and violence above her disappeared.

As she tumbled, her mother's cloak enveloped her, wrapping her in its comforting folds. It was as if her mother's arms were embracing her, offering a sanctuary of warmth and security. The familiar scent of her mother lingered in the fabric, evoking memories of a tenderly sung lullaby. In that moment, all the cherished sensations of being a child in her mother's presence flooded her heart, giving her an overwhelming sense of safety, warmth, and fulfillment.

Then she hit the rocks.

~ 33 ~
The Tether

"Are you alright? Can you move?"

A hand was on Catherine's shoulder and she opened her eyes.

"Huh, where am I?"

"I saw you from the roadside; you fell down the cliff."

The pain seared in her temples and she remembered banging her head. "Oh."

"Are you okay? Anything broken?"

"I don't know," she flexed her arms and legs pushing herself up to a seating position. "No, I'm fine," she was surprised, touching the sore but unbloodied lump on her head.

"Man, you must be SO lucky. I only have to trip up and I break a leg."

She took a look at the good Samaritan. He was a small balding man dressed in a suit. "Are you sure you're okay, I mean, do you want me to call an ambulance?"

"No, no, I'm fine. Thank you."

The man was hovering from one foot to the other hunched over her, and she felt a little suffocated. He seemed to be enjoying the drama of it all and although she was grateful to him, she was starting to find it rather irritating.

"Okay, well as long as you're okay then?"

"Yes, thanks," she got to her feet, brushing the accumulated vegetation off her clothes. With another glance he shuffled off towards the steps. Catherine inspected the various scrapes and bruises on her arms and legs. Her back hurt just below her shoulder blades but she was able to move them around without too much pain and was satisfied that nothing was broken.

She looked up at the window and then at the rocks below the cliff. So, the nun had committed suicide. A mortal sin. All those dreams Catherine had had of falling, and of stepping backwards off a cliff – they had come from this.

The thing was that the nun hadn't been giving up when she let herself fall. She had taken control of the last moments of her life and she felt free at last. She had made a choice *how* to die. She could have submitted, been enslaved, traded and abused only to die in chains for her master, or of hunger or disease; or she could fight and die by the sword there and then – both options would take away further choices she had. Choosing her own manner of death was liberating and empowering - and as she fell, she found peace. Catherine was in awe of the nun - for her bravery and clarity of thought. It wasn't sinful or shameful. It was a choice. And Catherine knew that, in this case, it was the right choice.

Catherine shook her head. When did she accept all of this as fact? The whole situation, the memories, the dreams - it might all be in her head. Maybe she was in the midst of a breakdown.

She needed another coffee and wanted to get off the beach, so decided to go back up to the road – a little bruised but otherwise unscathed from her tumble down the cliff.

As she was looking for another cafe, she passed a small library building which was in the process of opening up. Maybe that would be a good place to look for some answers – to find out whether or not these memories were in fact true. On impulse she went in.

Tynemouth library was smaller than she expected, being about the size of the other local shops in the high street. The walls were lined with books and it extended into what would have been the storage area for the other shops. In the back room connected by an open archway there were tables to sit at and the place was deserted apart from the librarian behind the counter at the entrance.

The older woman greeted her as Catherine came in and asked if she could help.

"I'm looking for information about Tynemouth Priory; do you have any history books on the area?"

"We can do better than that," said the librarian, obviously proud of her facility. "We have research projects and specific excavation reports for the site here in the library."

"That's perfect, is it possible for me to look at them?"

"Certainly, take a seat and I'll bring them out to you."

The woman came out from behind the counter and went into the back room, whilst Catherine followed and took a seat as instructed.

The woman pulled out some files from the shelves and a couple of books. "There's more here if you want to look at it, but it's all reference material, so you can't take it away with you." She looked at Catherine over her half-moon glasses with an accusatory expression.

"I understand." For some reason Catherine felt a little guilty as if she had indeed planned to remove the precious manuscripts.

The librarian took a long hard look at Catherine who was reminded of a mother superior. Catherine smiled nervously which seemed to placate the suspicious bibliosoph.

"I'll be careful with them, I promise."

"Of course," the woman put the files on the table and went back to her counter.

Catherine watched her depart then turned back to the reference books. Where to start?

She looked at the tomes in front of her – she'd always had a reverence for books instilled in her as a child. Rarely had she been allowed to watch television except if it was educational, her grandmother feeling books were 'better for the brain'. And having a library on the same block as her house, meant that membership at the age of 6 was something that she had treasured. It was a place she visited often and somewhere she had known she was welcome.

Catherine had a flash of the Saxon girl's reverence for books. She had been a member of an elite class being able to read and write in her day. Books to her were not only special they were invaluable objects which set her apart, and which individually took years to create. They were the equivalent of the leading-edge technology of the time which not only recorded information but also allowed it to be transported to new places. It was more revolutionary in her time, than the invention of computers in Catherine's. To the Saxons this small library was a palace of unequalled value.

Catherine reached for the oldest looking book and pulled it before her. It was the history of Tynemouth Priory. She already had an idea of when the Saxon girl lived – around the mid 9th Century probably – so that gave her a starting point.

She found out so much information – how Tynemouth was thought to have been a religious site right back into Roman times, though not enough archaeological evidence had been uncovered to say what the Romans had done there. A church had been there since at least the 7th century and there were many references to the priory as three kings had been buried there. King Oswin who was killed in 651AD. He was a 'courteous and generous king' of Northumberland known for his qualities of body and mind. Rather than have his soldiers butchered in battle he sent them home and gave himself up to his enemies, who of course murdered him.

Catherine sympathised with the man, "Hardly fair. What's that saying ... *no good deed goes unpunished.*" She continued reading.

He was then buried at Tynemouth and his tomb became a place of worship and many miracles were performed there as a result.

The next was King Osred, who died in 792AD, just before the first Viking attack at Tynemouth in 800AD. Osred was betrayed by his own nobles and lost the throne becoming a monk in York, then when he attempted to regain his title he was betrayed again and put to death on the orders of King 'Butcher' Ethelred.

The third king was Malcolm Canmore a fierce king of Scotland who was forever raiding Northumbria. In 1093AD his army met with William de Mowbray's forces near to Alnwick and in a fierce battle, 3000 Scots were slain. A chapel was built on the spot where he died, but his body was brought to Tynemouth for burial.

"So, there would only have been two kings buried at Tynemouth in your time," Catherine muttered, feeling the Saxon girl's presence next to her, as if they were sitting side by side.

There had also been caves under Tynemouth Priory. Local legend had it that they provided a tunnel from King Edwards Bay right under the river Tyne to Jarrow. The tunnel entrances had collapsed in medieval times, so no modern evidence of their location remained. However, there were stories of smugglers using the caves and even of a great treasure that had been found by a local boy who became a knight.

Northumberland had been troubled by Viking raids for a long time and the priory was raided in 800AD without resistance. The Vikings had destroyed the church and taken their spoils. Feeling that the site was too important to leave vulnerable again the monks fortified it against the raiders, successfully repelling a raid in 830AD.

Hours had passed and Catherine had eaten nothing since the round of toast that morning. The librarian had taken pity on her and brought a sweet cup of tea around lunchtime, even asking if she wanted half of her sandwich, but Catherine had not wanted to impose. She rather regretted saying no. She knew she'd need to stop soon but she was like an addict looking for an information high. She had to have more. Just one more file she promised herself and opened a dusty book entitled 'Tynemouth Priory and Danish Invasion of Northumberland.'

Curious, she read out loud.

Around 865 AD, the Danes launched a significant invasion in the North East of England, arriving in large numbers. This invasion, while seemingly lacking in organization and strategic planning, had a profound impact on the region. One of the primary targets was the Tynemouth Priory, known at the time as 'Benebalcrag'. It suffered greatly in the first major attack by the Danes in that year. The violence was brutal and indiscriminate, leading to the massacre of the nuns of St Hilda, who had previously fled Viking raids and sought sanctuary within the priory's walls, along with all the residing monks. The buildings, including the church, were destroyed; set ablaze, leaving many to perish either in the fire or by the sword.

The geographical advantage of Benebalcrag, being a defensible peninsula, would normally have offered protection against typical Viking raids. However, the scale and force of the Danish invasion were overwhelming, overpowering the unprepared clerical inhabitants.

Following the attack, the Danes didn't move on; they settled in Northumberland, effectively taking control of the land and establishing themselves as the new ruling class. They used the

*strongholds they had captured as bases from which they could
strengthen their hold on the region, allowing even more Danes
to arrive and settle, reshaping the social and political landscape
of Northumberland in the process.*

Catherine stopped reading. A shiver ran down her spine
and she shook her head to clear it. So the attack that she had
seen that very morning had happened – just as she had
envisioned it. She had found what she had been looking for.

The history books proved that it had all happened exactly
the way she had seen it. Either that or she had now lost her
mind completely.

Catherine stood in the doorway of the library, feeling numb
and that, somehow, the world had shifted sideways. The overly
familiar Tynemouth main street seemed overlaid with layers
upon layers of history. She became aware of the multitudes of
feet that had walked up and down that street over untold
centuries. From iron age muddy paths to Romans setting up
camp, from monks building a priory, to medieval markets –
generation after generation all walking in the same footsteps as
those that came before.

The feeling was overwhelming and she leant against the
door post totally lost in the moment.

The tower, the Vikings, the war with the Scots, even the
Danish invasion. Everything that she had seen as a Saxon girl
over a thousand years before, had occurred in reality.

"Excuse me."

Catherine looked up to see a stranger gesturing that he
wanted to go into the library. She mumbled a quick, "Sorry,"
and stepped out of the way. Then, unaware that she had even
started walking, her feet took her towards the priory.

Lost in thought she paid the entrance fee, smiling without
mirth at the attendant who seemed uninterested in her

presence, and she walked through the imposing medieval gates.

It all looked so different now. The ruins in the wrong places. The decapitated church too big and too modern. None of the Saxon buildings remained, not even an outline. The landscape and the rise and fall of the earthworks had a strong familiarity though. She could picture the pottery kiln and the refectory, the smithy, the hospital and the stores. It all seemed so sad, so lost, so futile. It was all wiped clean away by the more modern Medieval settlement.

Catherine went to the spot that she had seen the Saxon girl's lover die, half expecting to see bones, or maybe even the stone snake. "Ammonite," Catherine corrected herself, "it was an ammonite."

There was nothing but manicured grass.

"Of course, don't be so stupid Catherine."

What had Bastian said - that maybe these memories of a past life were trying to teach her something in this life, but what?

The Saxon girl was a fighter, she knew what she wanted, she believed in herself right up to the end. Even though it meant her death she lived every moment. Whereas Catherine was always getting ready for the next stage of her life. As a child she studied to get good grades, so that she could go to college. At college she studied hard so that she could get a good job. A job that would allow her to get a flat, and eventually a better job and more money, a good pension, a peaceful retirement and then ... what? At what point had she ever planned to live and enjoy her life? To appreciate what she already had.

Catherine turned towards the ruined medieval church walls on the site of the Saxon church that she had watched burn that very morning.

The Saxon girl was loved, she had a sense of herself that Catherine never had. When that girl was being abused, she fought her way out and changed her whole life by going to war. That was so brave and something Catherine couldn't even imagine doing herself. Even when she had everything she needed, the Saxon girl still wanted freedom to choose her own path. She wanted to be on her own but she never felt alone. Catherine on the other hand had never been abused, she had been given everything on a platter. A roof over her head, three meals a day, a good education, a sense of self and control over her own future. And yet she had felt lonely her whole life, alone and unconnected. And when people tried to get close to her, she couldn't make that link. She seemed to shun those that showed any affection towards her because they were wrong to care. Was that what she had done with Edward?

Catherine turned her back on the modern ruins and towards the one thing that hadn't changed. The cliffs.

She seemed to be seeing herself from the outside and pitied what she saw. A shell-like creature, unloved, unwanted, and unnoticed. Her grandmother had said it so often - she was a *'waste of space and a burden to her family'* and had indeed ultimately amounted to nothing.

In a heavy daze, and feeling hopeless, she walked towards the edge, at the spot that she now remembered jumping from. She could see someone was already there.

The Saxon girl stood in front of her at the very edge, facing the sea. She turned to face Catherine just as she had done during the attack so many centuries ago. She stretched out her arms and she smiled. So at peace, so serene. Catherine watched mutely as the girl tilted backwards, a peaceful look in her eyes and a smile on her lips as she took control of her destiny and made her final decision.

Before she could fall though, she faded into mist.

Across the water and along the coastline was the constant movement of the waves. The beauty of the blue sky, as it joined the ocean at the horizon, filled Catherine's heart as the salt tang of the wind nudged her towards the edge. She noticed all the minute details around her: from the sunlight as it glinted across the distant water and the tiny white cloud which alone sat unmoving in the sky. She could feel the waves below swell and crash on the rocks, their ceaseless rhythm a testament to nature's unyielding power. The water was clear - enormous dark boulders visible below the surface, looking like ancient monsters clawing their way upwards. This was her recurring dream, where sometimes she fell and sometimes, she became a bird taking flight. Being in that spot, at that time, felt right and somehow destined.

Is this it? Is this what my subconscious wants me to do. Choose oblivion over a life without love?

~ 34 ~
Death

Dying was not the end of Merwynn. As everything faded to black, she experienced no abrupt halt that she might have expected. Instead, she felt like she was being squeezed through the hole of an hourglass leaving one world behind her and opening up to something new. Everything around her melted away like a wax candle in front of a fire.

As she was released from the last tethers of her body, everything opened up. She was floating free, although still in darkness. All confines of her limbs, flesh, skin and bone, were gone. She had never realised how trapped she had been. The freedom was intoxicating and had she still had a mouth she would have smiled or if she had had a voice she would have laughed. Instead, she just had an overwhelming sense of joy and peace. She stayed that way, in contentment for some time, it could have been moments, years, or centuries, time had no meaning there.

Then she realised that it was only dark because she had no eyes to see with. Instead she opened herself up and reached out with her feelings. In that moment, all of existence unfolded and she could 'see' everything, she knew everything, she was everything. She had been one tiny drop of water but now she was the boundless ocean.

With that revelation, she knew the love and the hate, the fears and the joys of anything that had energy. She knew how a candle felt about being a candle, how proud it was of its flame. How a blade of grass yearned to push itself up through the soil and the joy it knew at reaching the sunshine. How a bird elated in that leap into the air, knowing their wings would carry them. The grand slow pride of a tree as it gazed over the manic smaller creatures around it. Not thoughts, but feelings, the tiny pull of energy within every physical thing.

She knew and remembered every detail of every life that had existed on earth. She remembered how it was to lope as a vixen through the undergrowth of a forest. The satisfying grip of the earth under her claws as she ran, the balance of her tail and the joy of the chase even while feeling the growling ache of hunger in her fox's belly. At the same time, she knew the panic of the hare, how she trusted her powerful legs to escape the predator, the fear of being caught, and the hope that at least she was leading it away from her babies. Merwynn could feel that same fox, at the end of its life caught in a trap of some fashion, which cut into her back legs. She had tried biting through the trap with her sharp little teeth and tasted her own blood hot on her tongue. She had been too tired to continue and whimpering, she laid her head down to rest. Death had come over her then like a blanket, as her body was released and she was once again set free.

She could even remember the life of the small, coiled creature that had died so many millions of years before and given its body up to create the fossil that was such a prized possession of Merwynn's.

So many lives and she remembered them all. She understood how each and every human religion had come to believe what they did, and they were all right in their own ways. The Christians were right in that this was Heaven, but also the Vikings were right too as they were surrounded by their friends in the halls of Valhalla. It didn't matter what this was called, in truth it didn't have a name, for names are the domain of the living. They were only fighting about semantics – the writings of people trying to define what Merwynn now knew. Trying to put rules and definitions on something that could not be contained. All they could do was focus on their own realm of experience, their own tiny view of this enormity, but they were all missing the big picture. Disputing over 'god' or 'gods' was like each faith arguing over the petals of a single bloom in a meadow full of flowers.

So futile. Such wasted energy. And yet it was their energy to waste.

This was not one thing to be contained with words. This was everything that had ever been. Everything, and everyone - including all those that had ever come before her. There were a multitude of those that she could now remember but had not known in Merwynn's lifetime. Then were others that she recognised – others that had died before her. The stern nuns, and gentle monks who had perished at the hands of the Danish invaders, the gruff strong friends who had died in battles against the Gaels and Picts, even those strange blue painted men she had killed herself. The king, Cináed mac Ailpin, was there alongside villagers she had known growing up who had died of illness or violence, two of her siblings who she had not seen since leaving home and even the sweet Gwenhild. Each were part of her, and their lives were remembered as if her own.

Merwynn could even feel her mother, the first person she had lost in life, who radiated around her and, now as equals, they enveloped each other in love. They were all her as well. They were all part of the whole. Merwynn also felt the little girl from the haystack and with the recognition came the memories of her life too. Cwen had suffered greatly at the hands of the Vikings, passed from one group to another before dying of disease only a year later. Yet despite her pain and miserable end, she was there with Merwynn with no bitterness – Cwen welcomed Merwynn with understanding and complete acceptance. She too was part of the whole and that one short life she had led was only a small part of their existence. With almost a sob Merwynn absorbed the little girl into her like a hug of welcome reunification. All was forgiven.

In that absolution, the deep sense of guilt Merwyyn always carried with her dissipated. She was home and she was healed.

She even remembered the lives of the heathens that she had battled, and the Vikings that had raided. So hated in life, she could see now that they were not hateful in themselves, just a more brutal and selfish race who believed that might and glory were all that mattered. They too were part of this ocean, their love for their children and their pride and passion for their families shone through. They too were forgiven and accepted.

In recognising all those she had been close to in life, Merwynn realised that everyone who came behind her would find out, no matter what they had believed in their lifetime. That the power that the living called 'God' was not a separate being, or an entity that looked down on us from afar. God was inside us all, inside everything, separated for a moment whilst encased in a new shell. Each of them, however, was still part of the whole, and would be again, and again, for as long as there was energy and matter.

As soon as Merwynn understood that, Merwynn was no more.

She began to twist, to reshape and reform - as if she was being pushed into a funnel. She didn't want to let go of the feeling so she pulled as much into her as she could and allowed herself to slide into another life.

～ 35 ～

The Precipice

Catherine took a step forward and looked downwards over the edge of the cliff.

"No," the Saxon girl's voice said, "that's not the way."

Without turning, Catherine hesitated. Then she sighed and sat down heavily on the grass. She sat looking out across the ocean, the timeless, changeless scene that connected them. "I don't know what I have to live for."

"Yes, you do. Stop fighting it, and let it come to you."

Catherine wanted answers, she needed to understand what had happened to her, why it always went so wrong. It was a matter of life and death now. This time she would not hold back. As the waves below her undulated and the world breathed deeply, Catherine closed her eyes, willing her body to relax.

She visualised the staircase, and her hand reaching for the handle, but this time she didn't hesitate. She threw open the door so hard that it crashed against the back wall. The barrier collapsed and the door splintered to dust. Then a gust of wind blew through the stairwell and the debris was blown away in the breeze.

In a flash all of Merwynn's existence flooded into her memory. From her first steps holding onto her mother's finger, to cradling her baby sister and feeling that bitter-sweet love mixed with the grief. From the longing looks and sweet touch of Adalbert's grooming, to his abuse and the exploding pain as his fists met her belly. Jumping in terror at every bell which reminded her of the haystack and living at the whim of those who took power. Then being one of many, growing strong and fearless, fighting with an army, taking their lands back from the heathens. The delicious control she had of Hengist and the fury of his betrayal, and then the sweet love of Gwenhild that threatened to tame her again. From birth to death. And throughout it all, a sense of being loved and needed and wanted. It was as if Merwynn had a boulder inside of her, a rock that she stood on that held her firm, no matter what wild seas pounded on her.

Catherine opened her eyes, with tears rolling down her cheeks, and looked at the red headed, freckled woman who sat beside her.

"I never had that ..." Catherine faltered, "that ... love. Your mother ..." She swallowed hard. "My mum never loved me." Finally, she had said it out loud.

"Why do you think that might be?"

"She never had a reason, just didn't care about me at all."

"Everyone has a reason for what they do, even if the reasoning is flawed." Merwynn said as she looked straight into Catherine's eyes. "We have to understand our past, so that we can learn from it and let it go. So we can be free to move forward into our future."

Catherine shrugged her shoulders.

She could feel a hole in her chest and she felt a sharp pain where her heart should have been. "How are you not angry, how do you not hate Adalbert, and Hengist, and the raiders?"

"To hate another human being is like hating yourself. It's futile and a waste of energy. Like one finger of your hand despising another," Merwynn said. "We're all part of the whole. Those that do not love in life take no sense of themselves away with them. For them death would seem like the end, for others - who have only hate - it might seem far worse. Either way, everything that they were, would be lost. In the end, love is all there is, and it is all that ultimately follows with us."

Catherine picked a bit of grass and let it fall between her fingers, deep in thought. She thought of Cwen under the haystack and the all-consuming guilt that Merwynn had carried with her. With a stab of shame she recognised the hurt that she herself had caused Edward. She had pulled away when he needed her most. She remembered with deep sorrow his voice when he told her about Fiona's attempted suicide. Catherine had run away like a coward, rather than give him the support he needed. He was probably better off without her. What a useless girlfriend she was. The thought felt like a stab in her heart and her breath staccato-ed.

"You were not to know," Merwynn said, "you had your own journey to go on. And how can you help anyone if you can't help yourself? You have to be standing on firm ground before you can reach out a hand to pull someone else up."

Catherine nodded.

"It is not too late for that. You still have time to make amends. Always. If Cwen could forgive me than anything is possible."

Catherine nodded again, though she still couldn't see him ever wanting to talk to her again. She inhaled deeply as she remembered Gwenhild, her small hands and milky skin, the curl of her hair and the fleck of gold in her eyes. The details that she hadn't seen before. The depth and richness of Merwynn's life. Each conversation, every touch and caress. The sadness Merwynn had for the pain Gwenhild had endured, and the regret that she too had been abandoned at the end.

"Would you have done it differently?" Merwynn asked.

"No," Catherine couldn't lie, "I would have wanted my freedom too.

"Gwenhild never could forgive or forget in life, she took the pain with her everywhere she went, always waiting for the sword to strike again. Until it did. Such a waste, she was such a sweet thing. She had the voice of an angel but rarely lifted her spirits high enough to sing."

"So, we should all just forgive and forget, love they neighbour, and let them treat us like shit?" Catherine felt angry though she was not sure why. She remembered with vivid clarity the treatment Merwynn had received at the hands of Adalbert. At the same time she recognised his pain and misery, how his life was one long angry, self-loathing, midden of shame and self-harm.

"No. You have to love yourself, first and foremost. You cannot save everyone and it is not your responsibility to do so. We may all be connected but each life is our own to make the best of it that we can."

Catherine continued to pick individual strands of grass and throw them off in front of her. "How can I love myself? I don't know how. I was always taught that self-love was wrong."

"If you don't love yourself, you can't love anyone or anything else. Because without that you can't respect anyone else for caring about you. If you were never taught to love, then you may need to teach yourself. Go back to the beginning, go back to your start. Why don't you feel loved?"

Catherine felt alone again. She looked around but Merwynn was not there. She was by herself on the clifftop looking out to sea. The grass was whispering to her as the breeze bent it one way and then another. Why did she not feel loved?

"I don't know," Catherine said out loud.

"Yes, you do," whispered the grass.

Then everything came into focus. Catherine knew with absolutely certainty the piece of information that had been just out of reach for her whole life. The answer to the question she had never known she was asking.

~ 36 ~

Saving Grace

Catherine tapped on the door. Tentatively at first. Then she checked herself, realising that she was looking at the ground and feeling her stomach in knots. She looked up and caught her reflection in the polished coloured glass of the door. Beside her she could almost see Merwynn, head tilted and an expectant smile on her face. She was not alone.

This had to be done.

Catherine straightened her back and lifted her chin as she knocked firmly on the door with a clenched fist. This had been coming for a long time and, Catherine knew she had nothing to feel frightened of.

It was her mother who answered the door. A furtive look of confusion on her face. At first Grace looked like she didn't recognise the woman on the doorstep – the daughter she hadn't seen in over a decade.

"Hi Mum."

"Oh," said Grace, "we weren't expecting you."

"I know," Catherine pushed the door wider and stepped inside. She gave her mother a brief and unexpected hug and noticed how she was bone thin. "But I'm here all the same."

Catherine looked at her mother for what seemed like the first time. She was in the last year of her 30s, the same height as Catherine, with long dark hair tied back, and the same hazel eyes. They were almost carbon copies of each other – except that her mother had a nervous look that Catherine had never identified before.

"I need to talk to you," Catherine directed to her mother as her grandmother Eve stepped into the hallway to see who was at the door. A little louder Catherine added, "I need to talk to you all."

"Well, don't just stand there in the doorway then, girl, come on in, if you must." Eve clipped. "I suppose you'll be wanting a cup of tea." With that she walked with a clipped step into the kitchen and busied herself with filling the kettle.

Grace looked disturbed but Catherine put a calming hand on her shoulder and said, "It'll be okay now mum, it really will."

Catherine followed her grandmother into the kitchen and stood in the doorway watching her. She was not that formidable a woman. Catherine wondered how she had been so frightened of Eve for so long. Grace came in behind Catherine and helped her mother getting the milk out of the fridge and pouring it into a jug.

Grace picked up an elegant teacup, then stopped and looked nervously at her mother.

Eve sighed and rolled her eyes. "She's not the queen."

Grace put the cup carefully back in the cupboard and took out the plain cups and saucers instead.

Standing in the doorway Catherine watched the two of them and recognised how Grace felt. For so long Catherine had tried to impress her grandmother, desperate for the recognition that she thought might one day come. It never did though. No matter what Catherine did, it was never enough. She had given up trying years ago, but Grace never had – she was still visiting every month like clockwork. She was still hoping that her mother would one day say, those elusive words, 'well done'.

Catherine waited until Eve had filled the tea pot and both women had sat down at the kitchen table. "I need to tell you both something and I need you to let me talk until I am finished. Will you do that?"

"Well I don't see ..." Eve started to protest.

Catherine held up her hand to stop her. "I NEED to tell you both something and I NEED you to let me talk until I am finished. Once I am done you never have to see me again. Okay?"

Eve busied herself with putting cups onto saucers and pouring the tea. Without looking up at Catherine she replied, "Well I suppose you had better get on with it then."

Catherine stepped into the room and turned to face them both. "I know why you never loved me," she started. "I get it now. I know what happened."

Grace let an involuntary moan escape and glanced towards Eve, who sat straight backed and rigid as she stared with fury at her granddaughter.

"It took me a long time and a very strange journey to figure it out, but I suppose I must always have known. It was all there. I just didn't realise what I was looking at. Mum," Catherine crouched down at Grace's feet, and took her mother's hands, "I know it wasn't your fault. I know that you did what you had to do to survive." Catherine looked up to see Merwynn standing in the doorway a kind smile on her face. The red headed woman nodded at her.

"I am so grateful for my life mum, and so sorry at the same time for what you had to go through to bring me into this world. I know that you were raped."

Her mother gasped. It was like Catherine had slapped her. Tears filled her eyes and she covered her face with her hands.

Eve snorted, "Rape!" she spat. "Rape you call it? She was a little temptress flaunting herself with her short skirts and make up ..."

"Shut up!" Catherine stood up and turned on her grandmother. She leaned in close, her eyes dark and her voice a low growl. "Be quiet, or so help me!"

Eve shrank back and Catherine enjoyed the reversal of power. Never before had Catherine shown any rebellion to Eve – she never stood up for herself or talked back. She had been terrified of her grandmother though she was not even aware why. That fear was gone now. All Catherine could see was a shrunken selfish old woman, hell bent on always getting her own way.

Eve tried to stand up, but Catherine stepped closer and the smaller woman sat back down in her chair.

Catherine swallowed hard and kept her voice calm, "It was NOT her fault. It is never the victim's fault. How can you be so heartless? This was your daughter, your flesh and blood, and instead of looking after her you condemned her and called her names. You should be ashamed of yourself. Her life, and mine, could have been so different if you had only had a little love in your heart. Not only content to blame her, but you also blamed ME!"

"You were conceived in sin," Eve hissed through bared teeth as if chewing the words. "How could you ever amount to anything after that? You were always a disappointment and yet nothing more than I expected. You are the spawn of the devil. The embodiment of the deadly sins – prideful, greedy, envious, lazy ... and now wrathful." She looked as if she relished saying what she thought.

"You forgot gluttony and lust. And no, I am not. I am just born of a girl who was abused. What I am, YOU made me." Catherine was feeling calm despite seeing the hate in her grandmother's eyes.

"How DARE you," Eve screamed still sitting in her seat as Catherine loomed over her. "I gave you a roof over your head, I fed you. I clothed you. I gave you everything you needed."

"No," Catherine shook her head. "No, you didn't. You didn't give me any love." She stepped over to Grace and put her hand on her mother's shoulder. "We both deserved to be loved …deserve … to be loved. And we will be."

At that moment Catherine's grandfather, Jim, came into the room. "What on earth is going on here?" he snapped, "I heard yelling."

Catherine felt Grace's shoulder muscles flinch under her hand. At the same time Grace turned her head away from him. Catherine recognised the body language. It was the same reaction Merwynn had had to Adalbert in the last days before she escaped.

Very slowly Catherine turned to look at Jim, with eyes of murderous flint. Behind his shoulder she saw Merwynn with the same hooded expression as she reached out towards him. "It was you!" Catherine almost spat the words at him.

"What in God's name are you talking about?" Jim faltered, looking like he wanted to flee but his feet wouldn't move. He stood in the doorway holding his chest as if an icy hand had grabbed his heart. "I, I … oh for goodness' sake, you don't believe Grace do you." He looked at Eve with pleading eyes, terror gripped him. "She's lying!" he said, "I never touched her."

Catherine turned to Eve and saw that she was staring back at him blankly.

"You knew!" Catherine ground the words out at her grandmother. "You knew what he did?"

"So, I knew, so what? What difference does it make?" Eve straightened her back and crossed her arms.

Catherine opened her mouth to speak but nothing came out.

For a moment there was a thick silence in the room.

It was Grace who spoke first, slowly and painfully. "It makes all the difference … to me. You knew. And still you made my life hell. You were supposed to be there and take care

227

of me. Of both of us. But instead you let him … do that …to me?"

Eve said nothing. She pursed her lips, looked the other way and took a sip of tea.

Catherine was reeling – the man she had known as her grandfather, the one who always ignored her and kept out of the way, was in fact her father? Worse he was a rapist and paedophile – the worst of men. In the previous few days she had come to terms with the realisation that she was the product of rape – she had been determined to do that before confronting her mother – but incest was not something she had not anticipated.

Grace was gaining in confidence and volume. "Even when I got pregnant, when he finally left me alone. It was YOU that insisted I keep the baby and bring her up in the house. All the while calling me a whore, telling me that I was going to hell!"

Eve snapped, "It was YOUR lust, both of you," she jabbed a finger at Grace and Jim. "It was your sin, and your punishment. Yet I was the one who had to endure it. My own daughter having an affair with my husband. You disgust me. You both deserved to have your faces rubbed in it every day."

Catherine stood open mouthed in horror, her fury at Eve rising fast, but before she could speak, Grace stood up so fast that the chair fell over.

"Yes, at first I craved his affection because I never got any from YOU! He used to come to my bedroom at night when I was little and read to me, tucked me into bed. Would kiss me goodnight. I didn't know. I didn't know that fathers didn't touch you like that." Tears were streaming down Grace's face. "I was 11 when he first raped me, mother, 11! Did you know THAT? After that I used to wait every night terrified. Not knowing if he would leave me alone or hurt me some more. He said you would kill me if you found out." She looked to Jim still standing, ashen faced, in the doorway and back to Eve.

"You're evil. Both of you. Parents are supposed to love their children but you two ... You're monsters." Grace took both of Catherine's hands. "Please forgive me, I was so young and so wrong, I didn't know how to stand up to her, or how to be a mother." Grace took in a shuddering breath, "I am so sorry."

Catherine squeezed her hands – things were moving faster and more out of control than she'd planned for.

"Honour your father and mother," Eve cited her favourite quote from the bible. Then she added, "First God, then your parents."

Catherine found her voice and glared at Eve, "You are nothing to us now. You made your choice and I hope you rot together." With that she and Grace turned, hand in hand, to the door.

For a moment Jim barred the way, he was opening and closing his mouth as if trying to formulate words but nothing was coming out. His breath was coming in short bursts and his hand clutched his chest, his forehead glistening with sweat.

Catherine pulled herself up to her full height and went up close to him and hissed, "Get out of our way."

Jim stumbled to the side as if pushed from behind, falling heavily to the floor. For the briefest moment Catherine looked at her father struggling for breath on the kitchen tile, then at her grandmother.

Eve picked up her tea cup in one hand and the saucer in the other. She pressed the cup to her lips and took a slow calm sip. She didn't look at her husband or respond to his gasping appeal for help.

Merwynn smiled at Catherine and gestured towards the door. Catherine nodded once and led her mother out of their family home pulling the door shut behind them for the last time.

Outside in the sunshine, Grace stopped Catherine and they looked at each other for a long moment as if meeting for the first time. Then Grace pulled Catherine to her and wrapped her arms around her daughter. For the first time in her life Catherine felt the tentative love of her mother – like a small stone had taken root in the centre of her chest. Even the shock revelations of the encounter with her grandparents could not shake that feeling of connection, of worth, and of love. It was familiar and something which she recognised Merwyn had held onto to her whole life.

~ 37 ~
Home Sweet Home

"I like your mum," Catherine heard Merwynn say, as she waved goodbye to Grace.

"Me too," Catherine shrugged and shook her head to clear it. Her grandfather was her father. It was overwhelming and disgusted her - but also everything finally made sense. How he had distanced himself from her, why she grew up in tension, why she had never felt loved or cared for. She knew with intense clarity that it was not her fault, no more than it was Grace's and that neither or them had deserved to be treated the way they had. It would take a long time to come to terms with it fully - but knowing the truth was so much better than not understanding why the people in her childhood had behaved the way they did.

Ultimately, she may have lost her unwilling grandparents but she had gained a mother - something she had never before realised was so important to her. Knowing that she had the opportunity to now build a relationship with her mother meant more than the world to her and she realised that her self-worth revolved around that so much.

"She's very damaged though and it'll take a lot of time to heal properly. And probably a LOT of therapy. Me too, I reckon. But it's a start. She's going to talk to her husband tonight. Tell him about me, being her daughter I mean. Though I guess describing me as her sister before was half true as well.

Then, in time, I will get to meet my brothers. You know, it's all going to be alright."

"You're not finished yet!" Merwynn laughed.

"I know," Catherine smiled back, "I think this might be even scarier than facing Eve."

"You'll manage. Just get on with it."

With that Catherine took out her phone and dialled Edward's number.

It rang five times before going to answer machine. Not a good sign. Catherine was not going to be deterred though. She rang his home number. It was Fiona who answered.

"Hello?"

Catherine ignored the part of her that wanted to hang up and run, and ploughed on, determined to fight for love. "Hi, Fiona, how are you doing?"

"Rough but getting there. To be honest I feel rather embarrassed and ashamed of what I put Ed through. He didn't deserve that."

"What was it all about?"

"I don't know. I only vaguely remember taking the pills. I couldn't stop thinking about my past life. I wasn't sleeping much. I felt unattractive and worthless ...and just so hopeless. I started downing vodkas. I kept thinking that I would never find my 'one' and if I do that maybe my soulmate is a psychopath who will hunt me down and kill me."

"I don't think that's how it works, Fiona. I think if we have any connection with our past lives that they must be there to teach us something. To make sure that we don't repeat the same mistakes again. Maybe it is all to help you understand your mother better – to help you forgive her for dying of a broken heart. You were so young when she had the heart attack, and it must have felt like she'd left you behind - that your father had killed her by dying himself. There is a parallel there. But do you think either your mother or your father would have preferred not to have met?"

"No," Fiona admitted, "they loved each other so much and it shone in everything they did. You have never seen two people who adored each other as much."

"Well, if we are able to find a tenth of that spark in our lifetimes then we're lucky. Maybe our past lives are trying to give us the tools to recognise real love when we find it?"

"Maybe," Fiona sounded a little relieved. "It is good to talk to someone that doesn't think I'm crazy."

"I think you are saner than me, Fiona, and I am happy to talk this through with you properly. I hope that we can become better friends. I would like to be there for you and help you get through this. But seriously, lay off the vodka huh?"

"Will do," Fiona laughed.

"Good. I think I may quit too, or at least cut down a lot. Are you're feeling a bit better now?"

"Yes," She said. "One day at a time though. Ed has been wonderful. As always. Letting me stay with him and putting on a brave face. Especially as ..." she faltered.

"Especially as I ... didn't help," Catherine admitted. "I was going through something at the same time, and I couldn't ..." Catherine was pierced by a sharp stab of guilt remembering a moment on the clifftop when she considered following Merwynn off the edge. *What if* echoed in her mind – what if she had succumbed to that impulse? She pondered the depth of anguish it would have inflicted on him, particularly in the shadow of Fiona's recent attempt only days before.

"I know," Fiona said, her voice soft with understanding. "He told me about Shona. That she had been up to her old tricks. She got to you, didn't she?" Her words were like a balm acknowledging Catherine's turmoil without judgement. "I could cheerfully strangle that woman, the damage she has done to him. Even the police say there is nothing they can do.

Apparently lying about someone and ruining their life is not illegal!"

"No!" Catherine realised what Edward must have thought. Indeed, she had allowed Shona to get inside her head. To feed off her insecurities and drive a wedge between them. "It wasn't just Shona. I have been going through something myself. I want to explain it all to him, but he isn't answering my call. Is he there?"

"Hold on," Fiona said and the phone when quiet for a long while, before it was again picked up, "here you go."

"Hi," he sounded tired and drained.

She heard so much hurt in his voice, so much confusion and upset and she wanted to reach down the line and hug him.

"I am so sorry. I should have been there when you needed me. It's a long story, but I want to tell you everything. First things first though, I love you. So much more than I have ever managed to say before. I love you Edward, and I want to make this all right. I never believed Shona, not really, this all goes so much deeper and further back than that. Can we meet up? And talk? I need to see you - to apologise in person. I have so much I need to explain."

"Ok," Ed seemed a litter happier, and cautiously agreed to meet up that evening.

"It's all going to be okay," Catherine sighed with relief as she hung up the phone.

Merwynn smiled back, "It always is in the end."

Epilogue

Catherine stretched out her back, her second pregnancy was easier than the first but getting close to term put a lot of pressure on her spine. She picked up the two mugs of tea and took them back through to the living room, noticing with a warm feeling the two rings she now wore – a silver one on her right hand and a gold one on her left. Each of them meant the world to her. One given her by her mother as a symbol of her love, and one by her husband as a symbol of his. Each time she saw them she felt sandwiched by a deep connection and affection on both sides.

Sitting at the couch, Grace was bouncing her four-year-old granddaughter on her knees, playing 'this is the way the farmer rides', and making the little girl giggle.

Catherine often reflected back on the day that she nearly jumped off the cliff in Tynemouth. This happy loved little girl would not exist if she had taken that leap, neither would the new life growing inside of her. She came so close to losing everything, to throwing it all away. Had she been losing her mind when Merwynn had appeared to her? Although Catherine knew that Merwynn was not truly there, she still was grateful for the help that she had given. Catherine still imagined that she saw her sometimes. Usually when she needed some support, or a gentle reminder that everything was okay. She had become a silent companion, a grown-up imaginary friend, and a secret that Catherine kept close to her chest. Someone that gave Catherine support and encouragement and without whom she never would have managed to talk to Edward and explain everything that had happened.

Edward had been understanding though, and ultimately the experience had made them stronger. They had spent almost every day together since and their love had grown stronger and deeper. Edward was the best father her little girl could ever want for. Catherine now had that same rock inside her that Merwynn had known, that immovable and unshakeable piece of solid ground inside her chest - the knowledge that she was loved.

What surprised her though was how close she now was to her mother. Never could she have imagined this happy family, nor these three generations coming together and the love that they now held for each other to make up for times past.

Catherine sat down across from her mother.

"I wish I'd done more of this with you," Grace said with a touch of sadness and a guilty look.

"All in the past," Catherine smiled and passed her mother a steaming mug. It would still take time to fully heal.

"There was the one occasion, but you won't remember, you were too young."

"What was that?"

"Well, I was a bit drunk. It was when I'd started the nursing course, and I'd been out with the other students. I got home and snuck up the stairs. Eve was asleep but you came toddling through. We sat on my bed and I showed you my photos. It was just after I had grown my hair out long and you were running your fingers through it whilst I showed you the snaps."

"I don't remember any of that."

"You must have been about four or five at the time. Same age as Hope here." She tickled the little girl who squealed with delight.

"Photos?"

"Oh yes, my one and only trip away from home. The school took us to somewhere near Newcastle for the day. We toured some old castle by the sea. They had a funfair with a merry-go-round and even a puppet show. I remember that we played on the beach too. We even had a picnic in the ruins. It was a perfect day. I'd really wanted to go, so I'd forged Eve's signature on the permission slip. I'd taken tons of photos and I told you about each one, what I had seen and felt. We talked most of the night looking at one image at a time. It was so lovely to share those moments with you, to tell you the story of each photograph – to relive the whole day with you."

Catherine sat bolt upright.

Grace continued, "I'd only been 13 when I went on that trip, but it was a fond memory." She paused and a sweet smile crossed her lips, "I experienced a huge sense of hope when I was there. Like I had a chance of escape and somehow things would all be okay." She looked into Catherine's eyes, "Come to think of it, I must have already been pregnant with you, though I didn't know it at the time." Grace picked up her tea and took a sip. "I had to hide the photos from Eve. She would have killed me if she'd found out. But that night we lay on my bed and I told you all about it, and we fell asleep in each other's arms."

Catherine sat with her mug poised mid-air, her mouth agape. She glanced across the room to see Merwynn with her eyebrows raised and a twinkle in her eye, then the red-haired woman began to laugh. Bastian's words from that first session came back in a flash of memory. *As children we have a literal open mind, we absorb everything like sponges, and store it all away in massive subconscious data banks. But as we grow up our minds become more analytical and critical, stopping us from accessing that data.*

Catherine looked back at her mother, "Tynemouth?" she said.

Grace nodded in surprise, remembering with a smile. "That might have been it... yes."

About the Author

Mary Turner Thomson lives in the historically rich city of Edinburgh, Scotland, where the echoes of the past meet the vibrancy of the present. As the Managing Director of The Book Whisperers, a not-for-profit social enterprise, Mary dedicates her life to empowering aspiring authors to bring their literary dreams to fruition.

With a BA Hons in Creative and Performing Arts, complemented by diplomas in marketing, business advice, and literature/creative writing, Mary blends her educational background with real-world experience to enrich her storytelling. Her career journey has seen her transform from a business adviser and marketing consultant to a motivational trainer, ultimately leading her to the realm of writing and publishing.

Mary is the acclaimed author of two international best-selling true-crime memoirs: *The Bigamist* (2007) and *The Psychopath* (2021), both now published by Little A Publishing, and both of which have reached #1 in Kindle charts overall. Her literary repertoire also includes the comedic *Sociopath Subtext* and the children's book *The Zebra that got away from the Lion*, reflecting her versatility and depth as a writer.

Her first novel, *Hindsight: Echoes Through Time*, is woven with threads of her personal experiences, including a haunting yet true prologue rooted in a mysterious memory from her own past. This novel explores themes of resilience and recovery, influenced by Mary's own journey of overcoming adversity and finding strength in her mother's teachings.

Outside of her professional sphere, Mary cherishes her role as a mother to three grown children and finds joy and companionship in her dog, Honey. Her life is a testament to the power of resilience, a theme that resonates deeply in her writing.

If you want to find out more, sign up to Mary's website or find links to her other books and social media on her LinkTree link below:

Website: www.maryturnerthomson.com
LinkTree: www.bit.ly/maryturnerthomson

*"If you enjoyed **Hindsight: Echoes Through Time**, I would be incredibly grateful if you could take a moment to leave a review on Amazon or Goodreads. Your feedback not only supports me as an author but also helps to share this story with more readers.*

Thank you for joining me on this journey, and I look forward to hearing your thoughts."

Mary Turner Thomson